Love vs. Power

Kay Ferrell

Love vs. Power

Copyright 2016 by Kay Ferrell

Published by Shan Presents

www.shanpresents.com

<u>Text Shan to 22828 to stay up to date with new releases, sneak peeks, contest, and more...</u>

<u>Check your spam if you don't receive an email thanking you for signing up.</u>

Text SPROMANCE to 22828 to stay up to date on new releases, plus get information on contest, sneak peeks, and more!

Table of Contents

Chapter One 1

Chapter Two 17

Chapter Three 31

Chapter Four..47

Chapter Five..65

Chapter Six 83

Chapter Seven...101

Chapter Eight..117

Chapter Nine 139

Chapter Ten...155

Chapter One

"Good morning, everyone. Today, our main goal is to do whatever possible to win over Braylin and drive the success of our company. Usually, Todd is here to give us a pep talk, but since he is on vacation, we'll have to settle for the other half of our two-man CEO team."

Taylor was expecting another smug white boy, with more money than he could spend.

"Everyone, say hello to Ryan Smith. He loves to stay behind the scenes and knit pick your work behind your back." Morgan, the team leader joked.

"Good morning, everyone. Let's get to work," Ryan said.

Ryan was a beautiful specimen. He looked to be about 6'3", with beautiful, tanned skin, shimmering light blue eyes, and a gorgeous smile; he was just as handsome as your dream boyfriend would be. He definitely wasn't your typical white boy; he looked like a model. Taylor tried to downplay how gorgeous he was. Just like Taylor had told her friend, Alli, once be before, sleeping her way to the top was not on the radar.

"Who can give me an idea for the perfect direction we should take?" Ryan asked. Taylor lifted her hand. "You with the cute dress; what's your name?" He asked.

"I'm Taylor, and thank you. I think we should focus on putting her products in places where the average overweight person shops, Walmart and Amazon. In the past, our clients have seen a 65% increase in sales when going that route. We get an app with daily meals, exercises and fitness tools; her following will eat that up. Right now, her marketing team has her working on DVDs, paperback books only, and selling her vitamins in GNC only. This is 2016; in today's world everyone is into digital books, online shopping, and everyone shops in Walmart. We put her videos on a website with a membership fee, we put it on a digital platform, get her books on Kindles and digital book reading apps, we get her supplements and meals in Walmart, and other places that cater to lower and middle-class families looking to lose those extra pounds."

Ryan stared at Taylor; she pushed her hair back behind her ear and sat down.

"Wow! Does anyone think they can top that?" Everyone sat on their hands. "Fine, Taylor you're going to lead the team. You'll work with Morgan, Becky, and Tim to get this done. We're counting on you to bring it home for us." Taylor nodded in affirmation. "Thank you all, Taylor and team, I'll be looking to hear from you all by Thursday. Friday is the meeting day with Braylin. Let's have a good day." The meeting was adjourned, and everyone retreated back to their offices and cubicles. Taylor got up to leave, "Excuse me Taylor, it's nice to meet you. Your ideas were great, and you've really done your homework... I'm really looking forward to working with you." Ryan smiled with his perfect white teeth and dimples.

"Thank you, I'm trying to keep up with all of the men that are usually chosen to lead." Taylor said bashfully.

Ryan's expression changed. "Don't worry about that. While I'm here, you'll definitely have your opportunity to show and prove." He patted Taylor on the back and walked off. She went back to her desk.

"Oh. my goodness. Did you see him? Wow, I didn't think the Smith in Kragin & Smith would be a young and fine white boy, mm. Did I say fine?" Alli, one of the other marketing consultants, said.

She was a white girl who loved black men, and not the ones everyone wanted. She liked them rough around the edges. So to hear her compliment a white guy was weird and funny to Taylor. Alli didn't have a problem using her curves to get what she wanted. She was beautiful, confidential, and all about having fun… Taylor on the other hand, she was always considered a beautiful woman, but was all about her business, she'd come too far to lose it all on fun and games, and men…

Six years ago...

"Ma, it'll be okay. I'm not going to be far. I'm only going to Spelman, and it's less than an hour away." Taylor said, trying to console her mother. She was becoming weary with each passing week, the closer it got to Taylor's moving date.

Taylor was the youngest of three children, all girls, who were also Spelman College alums themselves. Taylor always felt she had big shoes to fill in order to follow the lead of her older sisters. Her eldest sister, Trinity, who was twenty-three, was in medical school to become a doctor. Her middle sister, Teagan, who was twenty-one and planning to go to law school to be an attorney, was in her senior year at Spelman. Her mother, Thandi, was an accountant and a single mother. Taylor's father had passed away when she was six years old, leaving a void in her young life at an early age. She didn't remember too much about her father, either; the older she got, the less she remembered. The only thing many spoke of beside him being a successful business accountant for a large company, and him leaving a lot of money to pay for the girls' college tuitions, was that he loved her dearly. Tay was a hard-worker and always had to be the best at everything. If she couldn't be the best at it, she just wouldn't do it. She was focused on her studies, but hung out with her friend, Janae, in her spare time. Janae was smart like Taylor, but liked to have fun. She was into boys and had been having sex since their junior year of high school.

"Tay, you just make sure you come home on the weekends. I don't know why you feel like you need to live on campus when we live so close." Thandi scolded Taylor or Tay. Much of her family had called her that since she could remember. Taylor rolled her eyes and walked out onto the porch to enjoy the warm, beautiful weather that the summer had been blessing them with.

Damn, it's summer already, and I'm going to college. I can't wait!

Tay sat on the porch and watched Janae walk down the street with one of her boy toys, Chris. He was a cute, but chubby boy, but Janae was smitten by him. You could tell just how much she liked him by the way she looked at him. They finally made it to the gate in front of Taylor's house, then kissed before parting ways. Janae walked up the walkway, then plopped down on one of the chairs that adorned the porch of Taylor's house.

"Hey chick! You look like you're having fun…not! Let's go find something to do." Janae complained.

"Wassup, girl. This *is* fun. It's a beautiful day, the birds are chirping…" Taylor said, drifting off before she could finish her sentence.

"But what? Look, I told you about letting your mother make you feel guilty for wanting to get a taste of the whole college student experience. Your sisters got to have their freedom. Now, it's your time. It's a damn all girl college anyway." Janae said, showing clear irritation with the whole situation.

"I know, but it's not about that. It's just the fact that I'm her baby, and I don't think she's ready…neither am I." Taylor confessed. She was a mama's baby to the heart, and she was nervous about everything that awaited her.

Two years later…

"Class, remember you have two days left to perfect your papers and have your slides ready for the overhead as well." Taylor's psychology professor repeated, trying to remind the class of the importance of this project for their mid-term grades.

"Taylor, can I speak to you for a minute?" Her professor, Liam, asked.

Liam was young, handsome, and unlike any of the boys Taylor had dated; he was the first older guy Taylor had ever been attracted to. Liam was 6'2, had beautiful, curly hair, green eyes, and the perfect smile. Taylor, along with some classmates had thought Liam looked like a model that needed to be stripped and rode.

"Yes, Professor Liam," Taylor answered, looking around the classroom, noticing they were alone.

"I remember the last time we spoke. You said you needed some help with the project. Did you still need it?" Liam asked.

Taylor smiled. Not only did she have a crush on him, but some alone time with "Professor Sexy" was exactly what she's imagined in her dreams of her and him.

"Yes, of course. That would be perfect. Are you free tonight?" She gushed.

"Perfect! We can get started now if you'd like. We can go up to the café a few miles from here." Liam said, pointing in the direction of the café.

Taylor followed Liam out of the door and to his car, where she plopped down in the passenger seat of his Volvo. They drove for a little while until they arrived at a quaint little café that served food and drinks and offered wide tables for studying. Liam found a seat for the two of them and guided Taylor into the booth. They picked up the menus and ordered chicken salad sandwiches and chips.

"So Taylor… Tell me more about your ideas for your project and what you've done so far." Liam asked.

"Well, my project is going to focus on the different aspects of attachment and detachment. I'm going to show the effect and the emotions of a child with his mother and one without his mother. I have everything done except my slideshow, and I really need help with it." Taylor exclaimed.

"Absolutely! That's going to be a great project. I can tell already. I have a few books at home with great quotes and photos for your slideshow, and I have a scanner. Would you like to come to my house to get that done? No pressure, though? This is strictly a teacher/student thing," Liam said with a blush.

Taylor agreed and off to his condo they went. She didn't think twice about what effects this event would have on her college career, or his, for that matter. They arrived at Liam's condo, and he immediately went to grab the books he'd told Taylor about, then walked her into his home office.

"Alright, let's get these scanned, uploaded, and get started on that slideshow."

"You don't think this is unfair to the other students since you're helping me with this project?" Taylor questioned.

"No, you're not the only student I'm helping with this project. A lot of students have never done a projector based project, so I'm trying to help everyone have a fair shot. Now, it's up to you all when it comes to the quality of work you turn in." Liam explained.

Taylor nodded in agreement and proceeded with the project. After about two hours, her slideshow was done and she was tired as hell. With cramming for a quiz for one of her other classes, and working on this project, sleep had been a distant friend. Taylor sat down on Liam's couch, and before long, had fallen asleep.

"Taylor! Taylor!" Liam shouted.

"Oh, my goodness, I'm sorry. I haven't really been getting sleep. What time is it?" She asked.

"It's 10 o'clock. Are you ready for me to take you back to your car?"

"It's the weekend. I'm in no hurry," Taylor joked.

A smile came across Liam's face. It was as if he was feeling the same way about Taylor as she did him. He couldn't help flirting with her; she was beautiful. Taylor had looks no man could resist. Her butter soft mocha skin had a natural glow; her head was adorned with curly, long hair. Taylor was all about natural hair. Her hair was soft and hung just past her shoulders. Thanks to her braces she had removed her junior year of high school, her teeth were pearly white and straight.

Her eyes were big and honey brown, and her body was amazing. She had a perfect ass and nice breasts, and she was about 5'7.

"Are you hungry? I have some frozen pizzas in the fridge and some beers, if you'd like." Liam asked.

"Sure! I can eat." she replied.

Liam threw a pizza in the oven and popped the top on two beers, giving Taylor one. Since Taylor wasn't old enough to drink, she would often sneak to get drunk with Janae and smoke weed here and there when they were around one of Janae's thug boyfriends. Once they were done eating, they relaxed, watching some Adam Sandler movie. You could see the admiration in Liam's eyes as he watched Taylor laugh at the jokes in the movie. She turned to catch him watching her.

"What? What's wrong?" Taylor asked.

"Nothing. Don't take this the wrong way, but…you're beautiful, and I have to admit that I've had a crush on you since the first day I met you in class. I know I'm the teacher, and I'm older, but I had to tell you. I'm twenty-five, and I know you're nineteen; that's only a six-year difference." Liam confessed.

Taylor was shocked; although she had a crush on her teacher, she would have never thought in a million years that he'd feel the same way about her. At the same time, nervousness set in. Yes, she had dated guys, but she was a virgin, and surely a man Liam's age would want to have sex. Suddenly, Taylor thought about what it would be like to lose her virginity to Liam. He was very handsome, and his body was toned with a six pack. She knew that from running into him at the beach during spring break. And his gorgeous smile would always have Taylor blushing.

"There's nothing wrong with that; I like you as well. And, no one has to know but us." Taylor smiled.

Liam instantly began to kiss Taylor, rubbing his fingers through her hair. She kissed him back, sucking on his lower lip. Liam's tongue explored Taylor's mouth, slowly opening her up for what was to come. He lifted her shirt above her head and unsnapped her bra, taking in the beautiful sight before him. He took both of her breasts into his mouth, sucking each one gently. Taylor threw her head back in enjoyment, moaning as pleasure started to consume her. She lifted her head and returned the favor by taking off his shirt and kissing his muscular chest. He had a tattoo of a quote on his chest, and Taylor rubbed her hand across it. Liam picked her up and walked her to his bedroom, where he laid on the bed, helping her out of her jeans. He removed his jeans, then climbed up to kiss her, he reached over and grabbed a condom from his nightstand. The sheer terror must've been written all over Taylor's face.

"What's the matter? If you don't want to do this, I'm fine with that. No pressure." Liam said sternly.

"Um, I've never done this before, but I don't want to stop." Taylor confessed.

"Are you sure?"

"Yes," she replied.

Liam pulled down her lace panties and kissed her inner thighs, lightly sucking on them. It was driving her insane. He threw her legs over his shoulders and started to feast on her pulsating, warm center. Taylor had never experienced this before, and she wasn't going to stop something that felt so damn good. Her head flew back, and her hands went into Liam's hair, scratching scalp.

"Oh my goodness, Liam!" Taylor moaned.

She was so into the moment that she almost cried when he slipped his fingers inside of her to make love to her insides. The way his tongue pleasured her clit had Taylor open and willing to go all the way with Liam. Taylor started to grind her hips into the thrusts his fingers were giving and the swirls his tongue were making. It wasn't long before the feeling had consumed her and she could no longer hold out on the inevitable.

"God Liam!" Taylor panted, as her warm, creamy climax exploded into his mouth, causing her to tremble.

Liam was satisfied with knowing he had brought her a pleasure that he'd hoped she never experienced before. He climbed up to her full lips and kissed her so passionately, staring into her eyes. He leaned back removing his boxers, removed the condom from the wrapper, and proceeded to slide it down his stiff erection. The look on Taylor's face had a bit of terror and excitement rolled into one.

Damn, I never seen a man with a dick that big, but of course, I've never been with one either. Am I really ready for this?

It was too late to second guess it now. Liam kissed her until she was relaxed. His fingers explored her again, making sure to focus on her clit, bringing her to another climax. Liam placed himself at her opening, rubbing his dick in her juices to help lubricate himself. He pushed in, but the tightness Taylor held forced him to work his way in for a couple of minutes.

"Ow! Can you give me a minute…okay?" Taylor gritted, trying to take the pain.

"I know it hurts, but I'll be gentle. Relax baby." Liam said with a comforting tone.

Taylor did as he asked and relaxed. The pain didn't go away, but he was finally able to enter her. He stroked her slow and deep once he was finally able to get in. Taylor was using her arms to keep a distance between her and Liam. The pain had started to subside from the stretching, but his length was another story.

"Ooh Tay, you feel so damn good baby." Liam moaned softly in her ear. His strokes began to speed up and became deep thrusts, as he neared his climax. "Oh my god, I'm cummin'!" Liam belted, as he filled the condom with his seeds and collapsed on top of Taylor.

I can't believe I did that. It hurt like hell, but it wasn't that bad. I could get used to this with him. I wonder if this makes us a couple now…

Her own thoughts consumed her until she fell asleep. The next morning, Liam woke her up with kisses, at 10 a.m.

*****

"Wake up, sleepy head. I have some fresh towels in the bathroom and a hot bubble bath waiting for you. Breakfast will be ready when you're done. Um…I'm going to take these sheets off of the bed. I'll toss them out, but I'll be back inside in one minute if you need me."

Taylor hadn't noticed the dried blood on her thighs and on the sheets. It wasn't a shock; Janae had told her all about what happens with your first, but she just didn't think it would be so much blood. She climbed out of bed in her naked glory without hesitation. Normally, she would be a little shy to be seen naked, even by her doctor, but she had new confidence.

Once she stepped into the bathroom, she looked at herself in the mirror. Physically, she looked the same, but emotionally, she had been changed. She felt different. She pulled her hair up into a bun and slid down into the warm bubble bath, watching the light swirls of blood float away from her body. She relaxed back into the water and closed her eyes. Last night was amazing, and she could only imagine how the next time would be, and the next, and the next. Taylor washed her body twice, then stood up to rinse off after letting the water out of the tub.

Liam had a gray wife beater and some basketball shorts laid out for her to put on. She threw on the clothes after opening the toothbrush he had sitting on the sink. Taylor made her way to the kitchen, and Liam had a spread fit for a princess. There were pancakes, eggs, sausage, bacon, biscuits, grits, fresh fruit, orange juice, coffee, and water. She was amazed at all of the effort, but she just had to know...

"Did you make all of this?" Taylor asked with a grin.

"Yes, I may have a white mother, but I'm a southern boy. I know my way around a kitchen. Let's eat!" Liam exclaimed.

They sat down and enjoyed breakfast together for the first time, and it definitely wouldn't be the last. Liam and Taylor were messing around for about two months, and Taylor was smitten. She felt like maybe Liam could be the one, and Liam felt the same about her. Everything was going great. They were hot and heavy and going at it like sex deprived fiends, until the shit hit the fan.

*****

"Hey bestie! I've missed you...you know you've been cooped up all weekend with mister you know who." Janae teased, walking with Taylor into the building that their psychology class was in.

They stepped into the lecture hall to find everyone staring at them as they walked in. There were a few girls rolling their eyes and whispering to each other. A couple others were giggling. Liam stood up front giving the lesson for today, not noticing Taylor walk in. She and Janae sat in the further row of seats next to one of the quiet students who never spoke to anyone.

"Damn, I wonder what's so fucking funny." Taylor questioned, annoyed with the looks and whispers.

"They know about you." The girl whispered.

"Excuse me? Who are you and what are you talking about?" Janae asked in her usual snappy, hood tone.

"I'm Anika. And I'm talking about you and Professor Liam hooking up. Some kind of way, you two were caught on a picture hugged up, look."

She pulled out her phone and showed Taylor a picture of her and Liam when they were in Savannah one weekend. They were walking into the movie theater. Taylor put her hand over her mouth and shook her head in disbelief. She didn't know what this would mean for their relationship or for Liam's job. Miraculously, only a handful of girls from the class received the photo, and it didn't get a chance to make it back to the Dean. From that day on, the girls in the class who knew gave her hell. Taylor never told Liam until the end.

One week later...

"Okay, class. This is the final test for this class, and it will greatly impact your grade, so it's best that you ladies study and focus on passing this test. There are no free rides." Liam announced.

"Yeah, I know somebody that's getting a free ride... on that dick!" One of the petty bitches whispered, but loud enough for Taylor to hear.

"Excuse me? Do you have something to say?" Taylor asked with an attitude.

"Yeah, bitch, you're sleeping with the teacher trying to get that easy A. I hope you pass... *hoe ass*." The ugly girl said rolling her neck.

Taylor jumped up wrapping her hands around the girl's throat, shaking her, while Janae looked on with laughter.

"Look, bitch, I suggest you keep your comments to yourself. You don't know me or shit about me, so mind your business." She said, as she pushed the girl down into her seat. She grabbed her things and stormed out of the lecture hall, with Janae trailing behind her.

"Damn, girl, you choked the shit out of that hoe. Haha! Nah, but for real, you can't let that shit get to you. It only makes them believe it's true. You gotta chill girl. Now, let's go, Tyson." Janae joked as they walked off towards Taylor's car.

The whole situation changed Taylor's outlook on dating co-workers, bosses, and anyone she was ever in business with. Her focus went on distancing herself from being in situations where "sleeping to the top" could ever be brought to her, but at the same time, kept her from being in any serious relationships since being at the top of her game was always her number one priority.

Present Day...

Chapter Two

Kragin & Smith was a power marketing company; it was known for making entrepreneurs and great products a household name. The owners, Todd Kragin and Ryan Smith, were best friends and had grown up among the wealthy in the suburban outskirts of Atlanta. Since they were teenagers, they had dreamed of becoming marketing gurus, forcing people to look to them for help with boosting the sales and stats of their companies. Although Todd and Ryan were jocks in high school and in college, it never stopped them from working hard to have at least a 3.5 GPA or from focusing on preparing for their company once they completed college. Todd and Ryan's fathers' were high-powered attorneys, who had a lot of connections and plenty of pull with the high rollers and celebrities in Georgia, so starting the company was simple, but it was the hard work of Todd and Ryan that kept the business booming and everyone happy. They started the company with five people, and it quickly expanded to twenty-five. Now, there are sixty employees, who were all handpicked and had top scholar credentials.

Ryan was always considered a pretty boy and the easy going friend out of the two. People often said he had a striking resemblance to David Beckham; they'd say he had that whole sexy, badass thing going on. He had the crystal blue eyes, dimples, and a gorgeous smile. His brown hair had natural highlights from being out in the sun. Playing football and basketball had his body ripped, and he practically had to beat the girls off with a stick. Handsome was an understatement when it came to Ryan, so as he got older, he started to use his looks to get women right where he wanted them… in bed and forgotten. He was definitely a playboy in his spare time, but that was only because he didn't find the women he dated interesting at all. They lacked goals, aspirations, integrity; they only wanted to be in his presence because of his looks and his money. In the beginning, it was fun and exciting, but once he reached twenty-five, it got old fast.

Now, he was playing the fence and looking for a wife to settle down and have a family with. He wanted to have a strong foundation, just like Todd. Todd had already gotten married and had a two-year-old daughter. Ryan's other best friend, Jason, told him to keep it moving, "he didn't need to be tied down with a bitch." Jason was the opposite of Todd. He was a handsome, black guy from the other side of Atlanta. He grew up in the hood and had to work hard for everything he had, but he did what he set out to do. He became an attorney and was a damn good one. Ryan often said that it was funny that Jason became an attorney, since he used to sell drugs to pay for his tuition. If you had never seen him on a work day, you would've thought he was just a regular thug with the way he spoke and dressed.

Ryan was used to dating white girls, who came from upper middle class or wealthy homes. They had never worked in their lives and their only goals were to look pretty on the arm of a wealthy man. He didn't care for that, so Jason introduced him to "real women," which is what Jason called black women. Ryan dated a few whom he found to have the qualities he was looking for, but there just hadn't been a connection. Once, he started to date black women, Ryan felt he no longer had a desire to date white women. They didn't relate to him. He had hung out with Jason so much that he began to speak like him, and he loved every bit of it. To his family and friends, he had become the badass, so Todd asked that he worked behind the scenes and allow him to be in the forefront for the sake of the company's image. Ryan agreed and worked from home, still putting his all into being the best.

Ryan had just come from a weekend trip with Jason to Miami,. The trip was filled with nothing but strip clubs, alcohol, and one-night stands. He had planned to relax at home for a few days to get himself together, but that plan was foiled when Todd called and told him that he and Meghan, his wife, were going on a vacation. He needed Ryan to cover for him for a little while. They were trying to land a contract with Braylin Lee, one of the biggest fitness gurus the world had yet to know about. She had all of the wrong marketing execs working with her, and Todd wanted a chance to show her what Kragin & Smith could do. Ryan agreed to fill in for him, but made him promise to make it up to him.

*****

"Good morning, Mr. Smith. The meeting will be held in the executive office. Here's your coffee and the reports on Ms. Braylin Lee. There's also a few notes on the execs that were picked by Mr. Kragin to get a shot at leading this campaign. Is there anything else I can do for you?" Lily, the assistant, asked.

"No, but thank you so much. I'll be in there in a moment. I just need to read up on Braylin and the execs. Tell Morgan to cover for me." Ryan told Lily. She nodded in agreement and left to do as she was told.

Once Ryan was caught up, he proceeded to the room where the meeting was being held. Morgan introduced Ryan to the team, many of whom had never met him and was shocked to see the Smith behind the name. He was dressed in slacks, a fitted tee, and a pair of Jimmy Choo sneakers. He walked in and stood behind Morgan wearing a smile and taking in each face seated at the table. He paused when he laid eyes on Taylor. She was one of the most beautiful women he'd ever seen, and from Todd's notes, she was also one of the brightest and hardest working women the company had to offer. Ryan stepped up and asked about the ideas the team had and who but Taylor, popped up with a whole strategic plan. Shockingly, Ryan was baffled. He had taken a liking to Taylor already.

When the meeting was over, he went over to let her know how he felt about her ideas and her leading the team. Ryan was shocked to find out that Taylor and other women in the office felt they weren't getting a shot at handling the big accounts and voice their ideas. Especially, since coming into this business. They'd promised never to overlook powerful team players, no matter what race, age, or gender they were. Many of their female classmates, who worked for other companies, told them about how the bosses would try to get sex out of them for better positions and more pay. Todd knew he had a gem with Taylor and was sleeping on her like a mattress.

Ryan reassured Taylor she would get her shine and that he was counting on her to pull through for the team. He walked off, still thinking about the way her dress hugged her curves. He had to get to know her and not push her. She seemed like she didn't take any shit, and he wasn't going to leave without taking his chances with Taylor. He walked back into his office and sat at his desk going over more paperwork, when Morgan entered his office.

"Great job today sir! I think you picked a great team, but did you really want to choose Taylor to be the team leader with such a big account? I mean, she's been here for a little less than a year, and she's led only one other campaign. She did secure it, but it wasn't a Braylin Lee type of account either." Morgan said, throwing all kinds of shade on Taylor's one shot at proving she can be as vital to this company as anyone else.

Ryan sat back in his chair and stared at Morgan with a look of disgust before giving him a piece of his mind.

"Really? Does it bother you that much that one of the new WOMEN will be leading this campaign? She has done a great job and has a proven track record here, so why shouldn't she get a shot?" Ryan asked, clearly annoyed with Morgan. "You know what, don't even answer that, and please excuse yourself." Ryan gritted.

Morgan left Ryan's office like a puppy with his tail between his legs, leaving Ryan to finish going over notes and ideas before finally heading home. He still had a slight hangover and wanted nothing more than to go home, relax, and think of ways to get a chance with Taylor. As he walked out of his office and out of the building, he spotted her walking towards the parking lot in front of him.

"Have a good night, Ms. Taylor." Ryan said, flashing his smile and dimples.

"You too, Mr. Smith. And please call me Tay. I'll see you in the morning, and don't worry, I won't let you down." Tay smiled and switched over to her 2015 Acura RLX.

"That's great! I'll see you tomorrow… *with your fine ass.*" Ryan said with a blush, whispering the last part to himself.

He climbed into his 2016 Mercedes CLS550 and turned up the radio, blasting SiriusXM Backspin station. After an hour drive, Ryan was finally home. He drug himself up the stairs and turned on the shower. His phone vibrated as he pulled boxers and a white t-shirt from the drawer and walked into the huge master bathroom of his four-bedroom home. *Who the hell is this?*

Todd: I heard about the meeting. Thanks so much for covering for me.

Ryan: You don't have to keep thanking me for doing hands-on work with MY company. You act as if I'm an outsider stepping in to help you. I think I'll be coming around more often. I've missed being in the office.

Todd: You're right, and you should do that. Lily said that everyone loved meeting with you and your personality, and that you're the "cool boss," I guess I'm the prick. By the way, we'll be back Wednesday, so I'll need you to be there again tomorrow.

Ryan: Cool!

Todd: I'll be back bright and early Wednesday morning.

Ryan: No rush, I'll be there all week. Have a good night. I have work in the morning.

Ryan didn't realize how irritated he had become, until he stepped into the shower and practically broke the shower door sliding it closed so hard. He had never paid attention before, but it almost felt like Todd was ostracizing him from the company. That only pushed him more to get his shit together. His employees needed to know him, and the people needed to know who really started this company, who landed the first account, and who really had the best track record.

*****

"Good morning, Mr. Smith. I wasn't expecting you back today until Mr. Kragin informed me you'll be in all week. Glad to see you. Here's your coffee. All of the prospect account information has been placed on your desk, and Taylor has turned in her marketing plan for the Braylin Lee account." Lily said, following Ryan into his office, helping him prepare for the day.

"Thank you so much, Lily. Can you please send Tay in? I'd like to speak with her." Ryan said, not looking up from Tay's plan.

There was a small pause before Lily spoke, "Taylor, sir?"

"Yes, let's call her Tay from now on. It rolls off the tongue much easier." Ryan replied smugly.

Lily nodded in agreement, then shut the door behind her. A few minutes later, Taylor stepped into Ryan's office, taking his breath away just as she had the day before. She had her hair pulled up into a messy bun and her makeup was perfect, making her big, honey brown eyes stand out. Like the day before, her peach dress hugged her curves, and her heels made her calves stand out like a stallion. Ryan licked his lips, then leaned back in his chair. He stretched his arm out to the chair in front of his desk, to offer Taylor a seat.

"Good morning, Mr. Smit. I see you're reading over my plan. I hope it meets your standards." Tay said with a grin. Her coyness seemed to turn Ryan on and being beautiful didn't help the matter much.

24

"Absolutely! That's what I wanted to talk to you about. And please do not take this the wrong way… you're a beautiful woman, so most men won't take you serious. They'll glance over your work, tell you things you really want to hear, and try to take advantage of you. That's not me. I'm going to give you nothing but the honest truth. I didn't become successful by lying to people. So, the truth is, your plan is completely…magnificent! You have made sure to cover every marketing outlet and scheme possible. I don't see a reason why Braylin would turn down this plan, unless she's just a plain idiot. There is nothing I would change about what you're wanting to do." Ryan gushed. Tay smiled and crossed her right leg over her left.

"Honestly, I've never seen anyone complete a marketing plan this fast. I just gave you this assignment yesterday. Wow, you're awesome!" Ryan said with pure amazement.

"Ha ha, I have to admit, every large account we have on the horizon, I go home and get on it immediately, so that when we have an assignment/team leader planning meeting, I can be prepared. Although, I'm never picked for the big accounts, I make sure I'm ready just in case. So, I've had this Braylin Lee plan done for about two weeks now. The only thing I had to do was schedule a daily meeting with the rest of the team to get prepared for the big day Friday. We've printed out the plans already, made a slideshow with potential numbers, and I'm ready." Taylor exclaimed, making Ryan smile.

Ryan knew he had made the right choice choosing Taylor for this project. He couldn't wait to show Todd that he knew exactly what he was doing and that he should stop trying to block him from the company. That whole bad guy excuse was really a lame one, and he knew that landing this account would make it hard for Todd to turn him down like he had done in the past.

"Thank you, Tay, for your hard work. Go ahead and continue your hard work on the other accounts and have a great meeting with the team today." Ryan smiled, allowing Taylor to excuse herself and head back to work.

Damn!

*****

Taylor was smiling from ear to ear as she walked back to her office. She sat in her chair and did a spin to face the city outside. This was like a dream come true. She had been working so hard to be seen as an equal. To feel like she was adequate enough to get the job done. And Ryan had been the first one to have faith in her. The small account she landed in the past was only because Susan, one of the other execs went into labor before she could work on the project and no one else wanted to come up with an idea for selling feminine hygiene products.

"Damn Tay, did y'all have a quickie?" Alli asked, taking Taylor from her thoughts.

"Come in here and shut up! We did not have a quickie, although the thought has crossed my mind. He was excited

26

about my work He was actually shocked that I had the plan done in one night." Taylor gushed.

"Did you tell him you had already done it?" Alli asked.

"Yes, and he was shocked at how serious I was about my job. Maybe my looks were throwing him off." Taylor questioned.

"You are a gorgeous bitch. Hell, I'd bang you." Alli joked.

"Ugh! What am I going to do with you? Let's go over to the café for lunch later. Now, get back to work." Taylor said, shooing Alli from her office while laughing. Alli gave her the stink eye, then sashayed back into her office. Taylor laughed at Alli some more then got back to work. She wasn't hardly in the business for slacking and wasn't looking to start.

Lunch rolled up before she knew it, and Alli had knocked on her door to let her know she was ready. Taylor grabbed her purse and closed the door to her office before walking off to join Alli for lunch. They exited the building and walked a few doors down to this café that had the best chicken in the city. They had any flavor of chicken you could think of... barbecue, jerked, baked, fried, hot wings, it was a popular place, to say the least. Taylor and Alli found a quiet little corner in the back of the restaurant, where they could gossip and chit chat about any and everything without bothering the rest of the lunch crowd.

"So, how does it feel to be the apple of the boss' eye? I can't wait until you kill this Friday and when you move up. Please take me with you." Alli teased.

"It's cool but to hell with all of that. What's the background on him? He's kinda cute." Taylor said with a grin.

"Oh, so you are interested in him? Well, he's twenty-five, he's very rich, and he's a bachelor. He and Todd Kragin are best friends." Alli said, spilling all of the tea Taylor needed.

"Hmm…single, that's good. I won't take it there with him, but I would feel bad having nasty thoughts about another woman's husband. And we both know I'm not going to even entertain the thought of fooling around with him. This is business." Taylor said with a stern look.

They ordered their food and beverages and were chatting about work and men, when Ryan walked in. He was standing in line waiting for his food. Just as he turned to leave, Ryan spotted Alli and Taylor at their table. Ryan walked over to them and smiled before speaking.

"Hello ladies. Still waiting on your food?" Ryan asked, still grinning.

"Oh, Mr. Smith. Hello, how are you?" Alli asked cheesing at Taylor.

"Hey, Alli, it's been a while. I'm good and yourself?" Ryan asked with sincerity.

"I'll be good if you guys give me a raise. Shit, I want a Gucci bag." Alli said, not caring what she said. Taylor kicked her underneath the table and gave her a look. "Don't kick me, I'm serious!" Alli exclaimed. Taylor shook her head and laughed as Alli went on.

"So, can I join you ladies?" Ryan asked, flashing that smile.

"You can have whatever you want. You're the boss." Taylor gushed.

Oh my god, did I just say that?

Alli laughed at the face Taylor was making, unaware the both of them were watching her. Taylor kicked Alli again. Then turned to smile at Ryan. He was red. He couldn't hide the fact that he liked the thought of having whatever he wanted from Taylor. The waiter came over to bring the check and focusing her attention on Ryan. He was definitely eye candy, and she was lustfully indulged.

"I like that. How about you and I go to dinner?" Ryan asked, still smiling.

"Um…I don't usually date co-workers…or bosses. Sorry." Taylor said getting up paying the bill and walking out with Alli in tow. Alli turned around and threw up her hands giving the "I don't know" signal to Ryan.

"Girl, why did you turn him down? Are you crazy? I mean, I know he's a white boy, but he's fine and in the dark you're both the same color." Alli said forcing Taylor to turn around and give her the side eye. "What?"

"I'm not going on a date with my boss. Not only is that unprofessional, but it's weird. What if something goes wrong, and he wants to fire me or something goes right, and he wants to fire me to keep me home?" Taylor said.

Alli laughed and shook her head at Taylor. The two of them together were a riot. They made it back to the office and went back to work, but not before Morgan pulled Taylor to the side.

"Hey Taylor, can I speak with you for a moment?"

"Sure, Morgan, what's up?" Taylor replied.

"I just wanted to give you the heads up that Kragin & Smith will be keeping a close eye on you, so you have to make sure you work hard to bring this one home for the team. Don't screw it up." Morgan said, walking off as to say the conversation was over.

Taylor frowned her face at the statement Morgan had just left her with. She knew that everyone would be eyeing her work since this was her first big account, but to tell her not to mess it up as if she had ever done so in the past, really pissed Taylor off. Morgan was always an ass kisser, and Taylor couldn't respect that about him. She only dealt with him because of the hard work and large accounts he'd brought in. She looked up to his work ethic and dynamic, but him personally…that was something else.

Taylor shut her door and got back to work on the three smaller accounts she managed, which was "Breeze," the feminine hygiene account, "Couture," an up and coming clothing brand for women that was backed by Beyoncé and Nicki Minaj, and a restaurant. After she'd completed her task with those assignments, she went back to the most important thing… snagging Braylin Lee and shutting down any naysayers that were against her. Even after what Morgan said, she couldn't seem to get Ryan out of her mind. His smile was etched into her thoughts and brought an instant smile to her face.

Chapter Three

"Feels good to be home. Thank you baby for a good time. I really needed that vacation." Todd told his wife, Meghan.

"You're welcome baby. I'll see you when you get home. Have a good day." Meghan said, kissing Todd and rubbing his cheek.

Todd made his way to the office to see how things were going. Even though Ryan was there looking over everything, Todd just couldn't let things just go. He walked into the office and was greeted by Lily with coffee and the plan and notes for the Braylin Lee account.

"Todd, I see you made it back. How was the trip?" Ryan asked with his handsome smirk.

"It was great. Meghan really enjoyed herself. How were things here?" Todd replied.

"Great! You came back just in time for our big meeting with Braylin Lee. Are you ready for this?" Ryan asked Todd.

"Absolutely! We have a few hours. I'd like to speak to the man in charge of this campaign." Todd replied.

"It's a woman. I chose Taylor. Did you not read her plans?" Ryan asked.

"Yes, I read them…but I thought they were from one of our more …masculine execs." Todd admitted.

"So, she isn't good enough to lead, but she's good enough to do the work?"

"Just put one of the men on it. We'll still use her ideas and notes, and he'll be the face for us."

"Why are you so dead set on not letting her be out there in the forefront, showing us that she is worthy enough for her position and eventually a raise?" Ryan asked.

"Don't act like you don't remember the last time we let a woman lead with a large account...she secretly started her own firm and took the account with her. I'm not going to lose again." Todd confessed.

"She's going to take care of us and that's final. I'll be in my office if you need me." Ryan said storming off into the direction of Taylor's office.

Knock Knock!

"Can I come in?" Ryan asked as he knocked on Taylor's open office door. Taylor nodded her head, giving Ryan the okay to come in.

"Today's the big day. Are you nervous?"

"No, I'm ready. I'm going to give it my all," Taylor replied with bright eyes.

"Alright. Look, everyone isn't as excited as I am about this, so make them believers."

Taylor nodded her head, walked around to her chair, and sat back as Ryan left her office. She was now more determined than ever.

*****

The meeting was started with rounds of specially ordered JuicyWater by Braylin. It was one of the many products she sold and was on high demand. Having them and some of the snacks she offered as an appetizer was Taylor's idea. Everyone was seated with Taylor sitting next to Ryan, who was at the head of the table, while Todd was at the other end. A copy of Taylor's proposal was handed to everyone, while Braylin was seated directly in front of Taylor, sparking a bit of nervousness in her.

"Alright, let's get started," Todd said, standing up and walking around the table before stopping behind Taylor.

"Braylin, we are here to wow you today and win you over. We'll have Taylor come up and present our proposal. I'm confident you'll love what she's willing to offer. Taylor…" Todd returned to his seat and allowed Taylor to walk up to the projector screen in the front of the room.

Her proposal explained everything she'd previously told Ryan and all the way down to the specifics of how to market her products, the best season for certain items, and projected numbers that seemed to peak Braylin's interest, as she leaned up in her seat. Braylin covered her smile with her hand and sat back, while Taylor ended her proposal with one of Braylin's famous quotes, "We'll make it if we try." Taylor sat down and everyone began to clap. The look on Todd's face let her know that it was a job well done.

"That was really great. I like that you've done so much research, and I've even learned some things about my brand that I didn't know. Great job! My colleagues and I will need to deliberate for a moment." Braylin said shaking Taylor's hand.

Everyone stood up and allowed Braylin Lee and her team the privacy they needed. Todd walked over to Taylor to pull her to the side so that they could speak in private.

"You really did an awesome job, wow! If she turns us down, then she wasn't really interested in the first place. You really outdid yourself. Again, great job, Taylor!"

Taylor turned to catch Todd giving her this look... one she hadn't gotten from him in a long time. Taylor brushed it off and sat with the rest of the team in the other conference room, to talk about what was said, and sat in waiting. Finally, Braylin's assistant returned and asked everyone to come back to the room. They all followed, returning to their seats and waiting on her answer. Braylin stood up and walked to the front of the room and began to speak.

"Young lady, you have truly impressed me, and believe me, I'm not easily impressed. This is the first marketing firm that has truly gotten to the bottom of my brand and truly understands what I stand for and why I'm doing this. To know that both of my parents died from health problems, diabetes, stroke, high cholesterol, high blood pressure, due to obesity... that impacted my life for the greater and so, wanting to inspire many people on a wider market, on a large scale, has been one of the most difficult challenges I've faced. But knowing that your company will work to schedule a fitness tour for me and get me my own workout/cooking show, that's damn impressive, and because of that, I'm going to agree to make Kragin & Smith my marketing firm."

Everyone cheered and clapped, shook each other's hands, and patted backs. Braylin lifted her hands to demand quiet before continuing to speak.

"Under one condition… this young lady here will be the manager of my marketing team. I want Taylor to personally lead each of the marketing campaigns that were discussed with me today. If she agrees, you've got yourself a deal." Braylin said with a smirk.

"Of course, I'll do it! Welcome to Kragin & Smith, I'm your marketing manager, Taylor Powers."

"I like your tenacity and your spunk!" Braylin said, kissing Taylor on the cheek then shaking hands with Ryan and Todd.

Landing this account was going to further the name of Kragin & Smith. Her name held weight like Oprah in the fitness and healthy eating world and having her alone was going to bring more money and clients to the company. Which meant a big promotion for Taylor and a new office because what Braylin was asking was placing her in a higher position. Taylor was on cloud nine; she damn near skipped back to her office, not knowing Alli was hot on her trails. When Taylor stopped to open her office door, Alli bumped into her.

"Damn girl! Don't be running up on me like that. What's up?" Taylor exclaimed.

"I'm so happy for you. My girl is moving on up to that deluxe apartment in the sky." Alli sang, mocking the "Jefferson's" theme song.

"I know right. Aah, I did it!" Taylor gushed.

There was a knock on her door. Ryan let himself into her office and leaned up against her desk.

"The team and Todd and I are going out to Zoli's tomorrow, kind of like a celebratory thing, dinner and drinks. I know that you're going right?" Ryan asked with that sexy smile.

"Absolutely! I deserve a night out. Plus, this allows me to get comfortable with the team who'll be working with me to keep this thing afloat." Taylor said.

"Um, excuse me. I didn't get an invite." Alli fussed.

"Come on, now, Alli. You know you're invited. You're the damn life of the party." Ryan teased.

*****

That evening, Taylor stopped over to her mother's for their weekly Friday night dinner. Every Friday, her and her sisters would go to their mom's house for dinner and wine just to keep in touch and catch up on what's been going on. Taylor's sister, Trinity, had become a cardiovascular surgeon, while Teagan was one of the youngest district attorney's in Atlanta. Thandi was still an accountant and was proud that all of her daughters were successful.

"Since I had a short day today, I made the collard greens, and Teagan made yams and cornbread." Trinity said, placing the dishes on the table.

"Well, I made everything else. What's been going on with you ladies?" Thandi asked while she finished preparing the table for dinner.

"Dorian and I got engaged! We're getting married." Teagan gushed, showing off her two-carat diamond ring.

"Oh my god, congratulations sis. I'm so happy for you two," Taylor exclaimed.

"That's so wonderful sis. Keenan and I are expecting. I'm three months pregnant!" Trinity shouted.

It seemed everyone had news. There was something good happening in everyone's life. Before Taylor could say what her news was, her mother went on with hers.

"Your stepfather and I are going on a trip to Rome in a couple of weeks." Thandi said in between bites.

"I landed the largest account in Kragin & Smith history. I got Braylin Lee to sign, and she got me a promotion by demanding I manage her account."

"That's wonderful!" They all seemed to say in unison.

"You deserve every bit of this. You have always worked your ass off for something like this, so I'm going to say it's about damn time. Now, when are you going to get a man?" Thandi asked, making Trinity and Teagan laugh.

"Really, Ma?" Taylor asked, with clear annoyance.

"Hell yeah, really. When is the last time you got laid? I keep telling you all work and no play won't keep the spider webs away." Thandi said, fanning between her legs, making Trinity and Teagan laugh again.

"Haha, very funny you guys. It's only been…uh…six months I think, maybe. Look, I just wanna be successful. Love can come later." Taylor pouted.

The rest of the night, the four of them talked, laughed, and joked until everyone was tired and ready to go home. Taylor loved spending her weekends with her mother and sisters. She was able to tell them any and everything and knew that they always had her best interests at heart, even her mother. The truth is, Taylor was too scared to date. Every time she found herself falling for someone, she'd get hurt in the worst way.

Her last relationship was eight months ago with Khalil. He played for the Falcons and was a starting running back on the team. Everything was going great until she found out she was his damn side piece. He was married, but supposedly, "separated", while he and Taylor were dating. His wife was crazy; she was coming to Taylor's job with the kids in the car, calling her job, and playing on her cell phone. Needless to say, Taylor learned her lesson about dating athletes. She didn't care how fine they were.

The day came so fast; it was almost like Christmas to her. She couldn't wait to see Ryan in regular clothes, to see his sexy blue eyes and gorgeous smile.

Oh my God, I like him!

Taylor couldn't fight it any longer; she really did like Ryan, but there was no way she could give in to her little crush; they worked together. They all saw where sleeping with the boss could take you. Most people saw it as a way to move up the ladder of success, while in reality, it just fucked everything up. Kragin & Smith was like any other job. They had their share of drama and scandal in the office, and most times, it was juicy. Like, how Lily came up from being a minimum wage mail sorter/copy & print girl to the assistant of Todd and now Ryan. It was no secret that she and Todd had a fling, but why not? She was a beautiful Latina woman, about twenty-five and had a killer body and a pretty face. She often talked about her love of fitness and how she hoped we got the account with Braylin so that she could work with her.

Then, there was Simone. She was a beauty as well. She worked in my department, low-level management of smaller accounts until one day, she got the chance to win over the hearts of a large account. She started her own marketing company and brilliantly stole that client from us, and now she's a competing company in the marketing game. It's said that her and Todd fooled around. He broke it off when his wife found out, and she took the client to get back at him. Well, it worked; he was in a funk for months after that. Simone left right before Taylor was hired.

Taylor got dressed in a fitted blue and black color block dress with matching cork wedges. Her natural hair was silk pressed at the salon earlier and her makeup was flattering, yet natural looking as usual. The doorbell rang, and Taylor switched over to the door to answer; she peeked through the peephole and pulled it open.

"Hey boo! I'm glad you changed your mind and decided to go with me today. I needed a sidekick." Taylor told Janae.

"Oh, you know I wasn't missing seeing this boss you were telling me about. If he is as fine as you say he is, y'all need to be hooking up." Janae said, as matter of fact.

"Here you go…let's just go out celebrate and have a good time please." Taylor pleaded.

"I'm just saying, do you think he has a friend? I got A1 credit and my own shit. Hook a sister up or something." Janae said with a grin.

"Um, what happened with you and Chris? I thought y'all were on the verge of marriage?" Taylor's teased.

"Girl, please. That clown got caught in some bitch's DM acting like he was the man. I told him to take his ass on. So I'm a free woman, again." Janae said.

She was beautiful and very confident. Janae had milk chocolate skin, medium length hair, and she wore in a bob. She was about 5'8, with hips and an ass that wouldn't quit. She had on a tight black dress and gold heels. Her makeup was flawless, and she was dressed to kill. The both of them looked like they we're models. They looked each other over and walked out. They climbed into Janae's 2016 Benz and took off.

"Is that ghetto ass friend of yours going to be there?" Janae asked, referring to Alli.

"Yes, she works with us and is a part of the team. She is not ghetto; she just likes to hang with black folks and she has a little flavor. She does not talk like that at work," Taylor laughed.

They pulled in front of Zoli's Bar and Grill and got out after spotting Morgan and Tim. They both had their women with them. Becky came with a few of her friends, and Alli had a couple of her black girlfriends with her. Todd, Ryan, and Jason walked in simultaneously leading the way to a private area they had reserved for us.

There were three small tables. Enough to seat everyone in the group comfortably. Todd and Ryan purposely made room at their table for Janae and Taylor, and Jason who also sat at the table. Everyone had ordered their food and drinks before they began to talk loud among each other. Janae was staring at Jason like a piece of meat. He was sexy to say the least. Jason was 6'3, had silky dark skin, a handsome face, and a beautiful white smile. He was giving Idris Elba and Lance Gross a run for their money, and they were losing. Janae smiled at Jason, slid her chair closer to his, and began a private conversation with him. The food and drinks were brought out and everyone began to eat. Ryan popped up and tapped his glass with his fork and cleared his throat.

"Attention everyone. I have to say a little something about why we're here tonight. This beautiful woman right here landed us one of THE largest clients ever and did it so effortlessly. You all have her to thank for the bonuses you will receive and the respect you'll gain from your peers. Let's continue to work hard to keep this client happy and make money doing it. To Taylor, I'm sorry, Tay." Ryan said with a smile, staring into the eyes of Taylor.

Everyone cheered and clanked their glasses together while saying "to Taylor." Once Todd announced that they were covering the bill, everyone was drinking and getting wasted. Zoli's had a pool table in the far back corner of the bar. Taylor, along with Janae, Ryan. and Jason were engulfed in a game when Todd walked over and wrapped his arms around Ryan and Taylor. He was clearly drunk, but so was everyone else.

"Taylor, you are really wearing that dress tonight. You look beautiful, and who's this? She's beautiful as well," Todd said, referring to Janae.

"I introduced you to her back at the table. That's my best friend, Janae." Taylor replied with clear annoyance.

"Janae, Mama Janae, ooh." Todd crooned, making Ryan frown.

Ryan walked Todd outside and stood with him until a cab came to take him home. He had called his wife to tell her to be looking out for him and to let him know that he had made it safely. When he was done with that, he returned to the table to get back into the game.

"So Janae, why is a beautiful woman like you single? I mean, you're an accountant for the big wigs. I know some young nigga is looking to make you his sugar mama." Jason asked with a laugh.

He had caught Janae off guard the way he spoke. Although, he was with Ryan, his whole persona and swag was different. You could tell Jason had spent some time in the hood, and that shit just turned Janae on more. She liked a hood dude that could hold his own, but also show a classy side, and Jason fit the description perfectly. Taylor was starting to lean on her pool stick, clearly tipsy after the two shots and the Long Island iced tea she was drinking.

"I weally like youuu," Taylor slurred as she rubbed her finger across Ryan's lip.

Taylor leaned in and locked lips with Ryan like they had been a couple for years. Had Janae not grabbed her, she would've probably tried to undress him. That didn't stop Ryan from kissing her back before she was snatched away. Janae walked Taylor out to the car, but not before giving Jason her number. Janae, along with the help of Ryan, finally got Taylor in the car.

"Thank youuu bwaby, call you morrow," Taylor slurred kissing Ryan again.

"Please get her home safely and tell her to call me tomorrow." Ryan smiled, slamming the door shut.

"Oh my god, Tay. You are so fucked up. You are going to hate yourself in the morning," Janae laughed.

But she was right...Taylor woke up with a hangover dressed in nothing but her underwear, and it was well after 11 a.m. when she woke up. Janae had been a good friend and decided to stay to make breakfast and to rub what happened last night in her face.

"Look who decided to wake up... did you have sweet dreams about your baby Ryan? I mean, he is fine as hell. He looks like one of those sexy, white actors that all of the women are always crying over. You lucked up and got you a winner girl! And the way you two were kissing last night, shit, we almost had to tell y'all to get a room." Janae teased, knowing that last bit would peak Taylor's interest.

"Kissing? Oh my god, please tell me I didn't. What happened?" Taylor asked.

"Well...you got drunk, and you were swapping spit with Ryan like y'all were about to fuck. Your hot ass told him you'd call him tomorrow, so he gave me his number to give to you. And, I exchanged numbers with Jason, or do you remember him?" Janae questioned.

"Yes, that's Ryan's fine ass black friend. But wait a minute, he gave me his number? I have to call him and get this straightened out before work tomorrow. Give me his number." Taylor demanded.

"It's on the counter next to breakfast and you're welcome, ungrateful heifer. Tell Ryan I said hi!" Janae shouted out to Taylor as she rushed into the kitchen. She came back into the living room with a plate of pancakes, bacon, and half of an omelet.

"Hi Ryan, how are you? That's good. Well...I just wanted to apologize for last night. I was really, really out of it. I didn't mean to kiss you, I'm so glad your girlfriend wasn't there. Oh you don't? You do? I admit I like you, too, but I can't date you. We work together. I mean, you're my boss, it just wouldn't work. But thanks for a great night, and again, sorry about that kiss." Taylor said before hanging up the phone.

"Bitch, are you crazy? That's a fine ass, good man you're turning down, because you work together? Don't worry, I know plenty of women who'd love to have him." Janae said, low-key getting mad that Taylor was about to let a good catch get away.

"I'm not jeopardizing my job for a relationship with my boss. What if it doesn't work out? Then everything will be fucked up and ain't no going back from that type of shit." Taylor argued.

Janae threw up her hands in defeat and turned her head back towards the TV, still shaking it at Taylor. They watched until Janae turned it off when her phone rang.

"Hello? Oh, hey Jason. Of course, I'd love to hang out. I spent the night at Tay's house. I gotta rummage through her closet and see what she has to wear, and I'll meet you there. Sure thing, later handsome." Janae bragged before hanging up the phone and smiling at Taylor.

"See, that's how you secure a real man, keep him interested. You're going to wind up old and lonely with twenty cats. You're too scared to take chances and that's going to stop you from truly being happy. I know being successful at your job is important to you, but personal happiness should be as well. Take notes honey. Now what do you have that I can wear? I need something tight to accentuate my boobs." Janae joked making Taylor laugh and nudge her arm.

Taylor rolled her eyes; she hated to admit it, but Janae was right. It had been so long since she'd gotten laid. She shook off the fond memories of the last time she did and helped Janae find something tight to wear on her date with Jason.

*****

Ryan was still in awe with the way Taylor was acting… like that kiss meant nothing to her, because it damn sure meant something to him. True, he wanted her to be sober the first time they'd hooked up, but he was still feeling her nonetheless. He expected her to call him and say that she wanted to meet up with him for a real date. He hung the phone up feeling defeated, so he decided to call Jason and see what was up with him.

"Hey, Jay, man wassup?" Ryan said.

"Nothing much, getting ready for my date with sexy ass Janae." Jason boasted.

"Date? Damn, is everybody *but* me getting some action? You need to have her convince her friend to give me a chance." Ryan pleaded.

"Haha, thirsty ass. I'll see what I can do. I thought she was down with you after the way she was on you last night. She came to her senses this morning, huh?" Jason joked.

"Alright, well I'll let you get to it. I'll sit here and get myself ready for work tomorrow." Ryan said before hanging up.

Ryan got up and walked out to his pool and pulled off his t-shirt and jeans. He was standing in nothing but his swim trunks. He stared at himself in the window. He was trying to figure out what he could do to win Taylor. He had to weigh her down, and he wouldn't stop until he got her. He was really falling for her, and he didn't know how to handle it. Ryan dove into the pool and swam a few laps before retreating to shower and change. He had a plan, and he was sure it would work.

Chapter Four

Monday...

Taylor didn't know why she was on edge today. She was running ten minutes late for work, which meant she arrived on time. She had spent too much time making sure she was cute. She had on a navy and floral pencil dress with matching navy and floral heels. Her natural hair was brushed up into a soft afro puff. Her pretty face and dimples added something extra to what she was wearing. She walked into her office, and immediately, started to regret not eating breakfast. She hurriedly got on her computer and started to get to work. She was getting ready to go and grab a cup of coffee from the break room when there was a knock on her door. Taylor looked up and smiled when she saw Ryan standing there with two Starbucks cups and a bag.

"Since you won't go out with me, I decided to bring breakfast to you. We can talk over breakfast sandwiches and caramel lattes." Ryan said with a smile, showing his perfect teeth.

"Oh my goodness, it's my favorite. How did you know?" She looked up and spotted Alli outside of her office smiling and waving.

"So what do you say?" Ryan asked.

"I guess it's okay. Come on in. Shut the door behind you." Taylor said while shutting the blinds and fighting her nerves.

"So, I guess that kiss was terrible the other day. You decided to go back on that phone call and blow me off. Look, I'm not trying to make you uncomfortable, but I really like you, and I believe in your work as well. I want you to be successful on your own. That's why I fought to make sure you were the one to deliver the plan at the meeting." Ryan confessed.

"So Todd wanted someone else to do it?" Taylor asked as usual, only focusing on the parts that she was really interested in.

"Yes, he felt like a man should take Braylin on, but he was wrong. She loves you. But, enough about that? How do you feel?" Ryan asked.

"About?" Taylor replied.

"About us. I know you felt it. So how about you give me a chance to take you out to a nice private dinner?" Ryan asked with this cute innocent look.

If Taylor wasn't as strong as she was, she would've given in to his boyish charm. Ryan turned her on, and she was fighting it like hell. She secretly imagined him naked when he first walked in, standing there with slim fit navy slacks, a pinstriped pink shirt unbuttoned at the top, with the sleeves rolled up, and a pair of expensive loafers. Everything about him screamed sexy actor. Taylor found it sexy and funny, especially since he was her boss.

"Um, I…I like you, but we work together. Things will just get complicated and awkward. If we didn't work together, I would definitely give you a shot." Taylor confessed.

Ryan nodded and continued to eat his sandwich and sip his coffee. Taylor had a feeling it would not be the last time Ryan asked, and to be honest, she got a kick out of him asking. In that moment, she thought about what Janae had said about missing out on her opportunity with a great guy, but she shook it off. When breakfast was done, Ryan excused himself to allow Taylor to get back to work. He said she had a lot of work to do to keep Braylin happy. Ryan left her office and took the elevator up to his office. He sat there for about a minute before Todd came in to interrupt.

"Hey Ryan. Glad to see you! You know I really thought you were just kidding when you said you were coming back to the office. We're going to get further with us both here leading the team. Oh yeah, sorry about the other night. Boy, was I wasted. I heard I hit on Taylor and her friend. I feel like a complete ass. I gotta apologize to her about that. She's adamant about keeping work about work. Anyway, I'll be in my office making sure that everything Taylor promised, we can really deliver, and that it goes exactly as planned for Braylin." Ryan gave Todd a head nod as he walked out of the door.

"That is one crazy white boy," Ryan said aloud.

Taylor was hammering away at her keyboard while on the phone with Walmart going over release dates and product lines for Braylin Lee, when Alli crept into her office signaling for her to hang up. Taylor finished her business then sat the receiver back down on the base.

"Aah, that was the last of them... all before lunch. I've set up launch dates, manufacturing schedules, and shipments for every market and book signings as well. I feel accomplished, your girl is the shit! Anyway, what's up?" Taylor asked almost out of breath from rambling on.

"Damn, did I miss the memo of when we stopped being friends? I mean, you barely spoke to me at the outing since you had your friend Janae with you. I know she doesn't like me. I don't know why, though, I ain't never done shit to her...I must've slept with her man." Alli said busting into laughter.

"You know what, you're an ass. Haha, no she never said she doesn't like you. She just thinks you're ghetto. I missed you friend. Don't be mad. I'll make it up to you. Tonight, you and I are going to go out for drinks after work. How does that sound?" Taylor said, trying to kiss up to Alli.

"Mm, I guess that's cool. The real reason I'm here though is, I wanna know how was that damn kiss? You and your lover boy were damn near ready to undress. You gave in?" Alli said with her eyes bucked, waiting for the juicy story.

"Uh no, I was drunk. I apologized and told him we can't do it. It won't work. We ate breakfast this morning, courtesy of someone telling him my favorites..." Alli smiled knowing she was the one who told. "And I told him if we didn't work together, then he would've had a shot." Taylor explained.

Alli shook her head in disgust. She still couldn't believe Taylor was playing these damn, "we work together" games.

"Girl, who cares? Ugh! Just get your shit together. I'll see you later." Alli said before slamming Taylor's door and walking off.

The day was finally over, and Taylor felt like she really needed a drink. She was tired of everyone being mad at her for wanting to be successful. It was her life, and if she wanted to be a prude, then that was on her. They had to just get over it. She didn't see anything wrong with getting up for work every morning and going home to a cold, lonely bed at night. At least she had Coco, her all-white Siberian Husky to keep her busy. She lived in a three-bedroom house, and she had things she never imagined she'd ever be able to afford because of her hard work. But the more she thought about it, the more she realized everyone had a point. She waved her hand at Alli who was meeting her at the bar down the street from the office.

"Hey sexy lady!" Alli said greeting Taylor.

"You're the sexy one. I see you've added some makeup. Planning on catching you one tonight?" Taylor asked.

"Well, you never know when you might run into something special. And I don't remember Mac lasting 8 hours on you either, miss. You've freshened up too. Let's order!" Alli exclaimed.

They started the night with four shots of Patron and Cîroc Apple Martinis to follow. They were buzzed by the time they noticed Will, who was nicknamed Sko, because of his last name Esko. He was one of Taylor's old flings from college. He spotted Taylor and made his way over to their table. Will was still fine. He was 6'4, caramel complexion, hazel eyes, and handsome as hell. Not to mention, his body was on point. Will owned several businesses and was very successful. Taylor hadn't seen him since college, but she had heard from friends how well he had been doing.

"Damn Tay, you're still as fine as I remembered. How have you been?" Will asked, rubbing his hands together.

"Sko! Hey, I'm doing great. I'm at Kragin & Smith now. How's business for you?" Taylor replied with a smile. She was tipsy and couldn't control her face.

"It's great. Are you going to introduce me to your friend, since she's smiling and holding her hand out," Will laughed.

"Oh, yeah. This is Alli. Alli, this is Will, but we call him Sko. We should catch up." Taylor gushed.

"Sure, how about now? We can make sure your friend gets home first, is that okay friend?" Will asked licking his lips and looking down on Alli.

"Hell yeah, my friend needs to get laid. Take her. I'll make it home. Don't worry about me." Alli exclaimed, staring at Taylor, who was scowling at her.

Will grabbed Taylor's hand and led her out of the bar and to an awaiting Range Rover. The entire ride to his place was a quiet one. Taylor didn't know what to say or where to begin. She was hoping Will would take the lead and make it easy for her to get through this night. Her relationship with Will was a short one. They had only dated for about two months, but it was two of the best months of her life. Will attended Morehouse across the way, and they dated at the end of their senior year in college, parting ways to start their careers. Will moved to L.A., while Taylor stayed in Atlanta, and that was the last time they'd heard from each other. They'd checked on one another through mutual friends, but this was the first time she'd laid eyes on him in years, and boy was he a sight for sore eyes. Taylor mentally fucked him in every way possible when she saw him at the bar and had only hoped he'd give her the pleasure of feeling him again for the night.

"So, how are things over at Kragin & Smith? They treating you right?" Will asked with a grin.

"Yes, I just got a promotion to a marketing manager position, and I personally landed the Braylin Lee account for us." Taylor said gleaming.

"That's wonderful! I knew you'd be successful. I came back to visit my family, plus my lil' sister is graduating from college now." Will said, just as they pulled up to his condo.

Will stepped out of the car and walked around to open the door for Taylor. He led the way up to the building. Once they were in the building, he pushed the elevator button and inserted a key to go up to 10th floor. They stepped off of the elevator into his condo. Taylor walked around in amazement of the sight and instantly fell in love with the view of downtown Atlanta and how beautifully decorated the place was.

"Wow! This is really nice. Did your wife decorate it for you?" Taylor asked, suspiciously, trying to get the scoop on his love life.

"I'm not married. I'm actually a bachelor… looking for a partner… someone who knows how to ride without even falling off." Will said, quoting Ginuwine's "Pony" song.

They both started to laugh as Will poured the two a glass of Ace of Spades. They nestled in front of the fireplace and began to reminisce on their college days. Taylor was staring at Will as he spoke and admired the form of his mouth. His juicy lips and the smoothness of his face. Will leaned in and kissed Taylor's lips so passionately, making her forget all of the dumb rules she had. Her hand slipped under his shirt and rubbed his six-pack. Sucking on his bottom lip, she started to pull his shirt up over his head.

Will slid out of his shirt, then stood up to step out of his pants. He unzipped Taylor's dress from the back and pushed the dress from her shoulders onto the floor. He marveled at the sight of her beautiful, mocha skin. Her toned body deserved to be kissed and made love to, and he felt he was just the man for the job. Her bra and panties were removed and her legs were propped on Will's shoulder as he dove into her honeypot face first. He sucked and licked on her pearl making her legs shake and tremble.

"Sko, ooh that feels so damn good," Taylor moaned as her fingers wandered through his hair and her fingernails scratched his scalp.

Will's warm tongue lapped at Taylor's juiciness and plunged into her sweet center, forcing her to throw an arch in her back as she lifted from the floor. She started to thrust her pelvis, making love to his mouth as he drove her insane. She looked down at Will and into his gorgeous eyes and almost fell in love. Taylor knew it was lust and the fact that she hadn't had sex in forever.

"Oh my god, I'm about to cuuummm!" Taylor yelled out.

Her sweet nectar seeped from her body and onto Will's handsome face, and he licked his lips, then lifted up onto his knees.

"You're so beautiful, baby. I missed this. Seeing you, holding you... making love." Will whispered, taking her bottom lip into his mouth and sucking it gently.

Will slid the Magnum down his thick, strong shaft, causing Taylor to lick her lips. She climbed onto his lap and slid down his pipe like a stripper on a pole, throwing her head back, seething every powerful thrust he gave.

Damn, this is some good dick... now, I remember why I was sick when he left.

Will laid Taylor back on the floor and placed her legs up on his shoulders as he dug deep in a circular motion causing her to yell out.

"Gawd baby, that feels so good. Oooh!" Taylor moaned.

Sko went back down on Taylor, sucking her thighs, kissing her pussy, and slipping his tongue between her lips. Taylor lost control of herself and her legs, she was moaning and shaking, gripping Sko's head, feeling herself on the brink of cumming. Before she could make it there, he reached up, flipping her over, and licked her from front to back, taking his time eating the groceries.

"Damn baby, eat that shit! Ooh, shit!" She cried out. Will climbed onto his knees and slid into her from the back, grabbing her hips with one hand and her hair with the other. He was working her over big time, and there was no getting away from the dick.

"Take this dick baby...shit, it's tight and so wet. I missed this pussy. Did you miss daddy's dick?" Will demanded.

"Yes daddy, gawd yes!" Taylor shouted, as he pounded into her punishing her.

"Shit, I'm about to cum!" Will exclaimed.

He pumped and pumped, filling the condom and making Taylor cum at the same time. Will got up and walked into the bathroom to flush the condom and came back to cuddle underneath the blanket with Taylor atop the plush rug in front of the fireplace. They fell asleep with the moonlight shining through the floor length windows and the fire crackling and flickering over them. In middle of the night, Taylor woke up to Ryan standing over her shaking his head.

"Taylor, how could you do this to me? I love you and you're just going to break my heart like this?" Ryan gritted.

Will jumped up as Ryan lunged towards him with a knife, stabbing him in the chest and turning towards Taylor.

She jumped up and realized it was just a dream...*what the hell?*

The next morning, Taylor got up before Will, got dressed, and crept out of the door. She took a cab back to her car that she left outside the bar, then drove home. As soon as she stepped into her house, she headed straight for the bathroom to run her a hot bubble bath. Taylor walked into her bedroom and pulled a pair of dress pants and a nice buttoned shirt from the closet and underwear from her drawer. She had about forty minutes to get ready for work and to get out of the house if she was going to at least be on time.

Taylor used twelve of her minutes soaking and washing her body. Fifteen of the minutes went towards getting dressed and doing makeup. She had co-washed her hair in the shower when she was rinsing off from her bath, so she was going to wear her long hair in its natural curl. She added moisturizers and headed into the kitchen to use the remainder of her time trying to get over the slight hangover she had. She popped a few Ibuprofen, drank a cup of coffee, and ate a donut, before her phone rang.

"Hello?" Taylor answered.

"Hey beautiful. I'm glad you thought enough of me to leave your number. I really enjoyed myself last night and would love to take you to dinner tonight at your favorite spot.

What do you say?" Will asked, sounding just as sexy as she knew he looked.

"Of course. I'll leave the office no later than 5, so is 7 okay?" Taylor said with a grin.

"No problem. I'll pick you up at 7, cool?" Will asked.

"See you then baby. I'll text you my address." Taylor said before hanging up.

Taylor sat there and thought about the night she had with Will and started to smile then that crazy ass dream she had popped into her head right after. She had the perfect opportunity to rekindle something that was so good with Will, but she still had Ryan on the brain. She had to gather herself before grabbing her purse, briefcase, and car keys. She set the alarm on her house, locked up, and headed out after texting Sko her address.

Taylor made it to the office and got right on her computer to get files and information in order for her first one-on-one meeting with Braylin Lee. Everything was organized and placed in a large manila folder labeled Braylin Lee. Taylor was staring out of her office window, like she often did, when the door opened and shut fast behind her. She turned around and noticed Alli standing in front of her desk with her hand on her hips with a sneaky grin on her face.

"Hey messy queen. How may I help you?" Taylor said coyly.

"Uh-uh, bitch give it up. You left with that fine ass specimen of chocolate delight. I know something happened, and don't tell me you all just talked and he took you home." Alli fussed.

Taylor got up and locked her door and closed the blinds before speaking to Alli.

"Okay, okay, sit down. Let me tell you what happened!" Taylor said just above a whisper. "Sko gave me everything I had been missing. Let's just say no part of my body went untouched. He made love to my damn soul and... we're going to dinner tonight." Taylor gushed.

"Yes, yes! I'm so happy for you. It's about time you got laid. Honey, you are glowing. And judging from the way you walked over to that door, he put that thang down on you. I knew that dude was packing, haha!" Alli said with a grin.

Taylor was smiling from ear-to-ear, which was quickly wiped away when Todd knocked on her door. She lifted the blinds and unlocked the door, allowing Alli to step out before Todd came in.

"Hi Todd, what can I do for you?" Taylor asked innocently.

"Hey, Taylor. I just wanted to check on you. How's the Braylin Lee account going?" Todd asked, glancing around Taylor's office.

She walked over to her desk and picked up the folder to show Todd she had completed her end of the deal she offered Braylin. She even had the numbers and everything in place for her.

"It's all here. I don't like to sit around waiting until the last minute to get things done. I like to get the work done, triple check it, then relax a second before moving on to the next task." Taylor said with a smile.

"I like to hear that. You're good at what you do, and I hate that it's taken me so long to recognize it. Also…I, uh, I wanted to apologize for hitting on you the other night at the celebration outing. I was really wasted, and when Ryan told me I hit on you and your friend, I felt like a total ass. I'm sorry for my unprofessional behavior." Todd pleaded.

"Todd, it's okay. You don't have to always be professional. We were out drinking, and I got wasted and showed my ass as well. It's okay, you're good." Taylor said with a smile.

"Thanks, well, I'll let you get back to your relaxing. See you later." Todd smiled before walking out of her office.

Taylor had never seen Todd act so… human. He was always going like a well-oiled machine, pushing everyone to work harder, always in his office on his computer, having conference calls and meetings. Todd just seemed to not have time for life. Taylor was shocked when she found out he was married with a kid. Clearly, he had time to do something. He was an okay guy. She started to see him in a different light, and to know that he was friends with Ryan, who was super cool, she knew he had to have been the same way once upon a time.

Taylor walked over to Alli's office, not noticing Ryan walking up behind her. He grabbed her shoulders like he was about to give her a massage, startling her.

"Hey Tay! I heard you were done with your one-on-one report for Braylin. I'd like to take you to dinner, help you relax." Ryan asked.

"Ryan, that would be great, but I have a date, and again, we work together. I don't think it would be wise for us to be out alone. Especially, since you're my boss. If the circumstances were different, I'd definitely give us a shot, but...I'm sorry. Thanks for the offer. See you later." Taylor said, walking into Alli's office. Alli glanced at her before shaking her head.

"Turning your future hubby down again, huh? That's okay. You have some sexy chocolate to tend to tonight. You giving it up again?" Alli asked curiously.

"Um, I don't know. If he plays his cards right, he may get to taste the goodies again." Taylor laughed. "You wanna go to lunch together? I really have the taste for some sausage, haha." She laughed again.

Alli shook her head at Taylor again, then grabbed her purse and Taylor's arm while walking out of the door. They drove over to Panera Bread and ordered soup and sandwiches, then watched as Todd was greeted by a beautiful, tanned woman. Her hair was blowing in the wind, and her dress fit her like it was made especially for her. They both walked over to Taylor and Alli's table wearing big grins.

"Sweetie, this the new marketing manager I was telling you about that's going to make our pockets swell. This is Taylor and one of the team members on the account, Alli. Ladies, this is my wife, Meghan." Todd gushed.

"Hello, nice to meet you." Taylor and Alli said in unison.

They chatted for a bit before Todd and his wife walked off. Taylor and Alli looked at each other before busting out in laughter. They couldn't believe Todd had gone through the trouble of introducing them to his wife. Especially, since he had been acting distant from the moment they started working for him. It only shed more light on the man he truly was to Taylor, and made him seem more normal than he had before. The ladies enjoyed their lunch before retreating back to work. They had several small accounts to manage, and to get offers and plans ready for potential clients.

Once Taylor was done with work, she hurried home to get ready for her date with Will. She stepped into her closet and pulled out this deep cut Chanel dress that hugged her curves like a glove. The silver dress stopped just above her knees and shimmered. The cut dropped down right above her navel. Her black Giuseppe pumps made her calves stand out and her long hair was curled to one side, falling over her left eye. Taylor looked delectable and she made sure her makeup accentuated the look. At 6:45, her doorbell rang, and she knew it was time for what she'd been waiting for all day. Taylor walked over and pulled the door open, only to find Ryan standing outside her door.

"Hey, Taylor. I'm not stalking you. I needed to bring you this report. Braylin is asking for a few more locations to push her product. Since the meeting is tomorrow afternoon, I took it upon myself to get the locations locked in and get the paperwork added to your file. This way, you'll be updated in the meeting tomorrow." Ryan confessed.

"Thanks, but um, couldn't this wait until the morning?" Taylor questioned.

"Actually no, since I'm going to be in late tomorrow." Ryan replied eyeing Taylor and licking his lips. "You look amazing. Damn. I'm sorry, I forgot you have a date. I'm going to get out of here. I'll see you tomorrow." Ryan exclaimed before walking off, getting into his car, and leaving.

Taylor pulled the folder up to her face and smelled the files that smelled of Ryan's cologne. She closed the door and went to add the finishing touches to her look. Shortly after, Will came to pick her up and whisked her off to her favorite restaurant. Cora's Soul Food Cuisine. It was one of the only upscale soul food places Taylor had ever been to, and the food was awesome. She couldn't believe Will remembered this place. The man was winning in every category, and she was still stuck with Ryan on her mind. She had to get him out of her head. Once dinner was done, they retreated to Taylor's house for part two of their sexual rendezvous, and it was just as good, if not better than the night before.

Chapter Five

Taylor's alarm went off waking her up for work. She hurriedly shut the alarm off to avoid waking Will. She got ready and left for work, leaving Will a note telling him how much she'd enjoyed him the night before, and that she had to get to an important meeting at work. She'd talk to him later. At the office, the meeting with Braylin went perfectly. Before they concluded their private meeting, Braylin pulled Taylor to the side.

"You seemed troubled. Are you okay?" Braylin asked, taking Taylor by surprise.

"I'm fine. I'm just excited about our working together. This is a dream come true." Taylor gushed, brushing off her question.

"Honestly, honey, what's wrong. This will stay between us. What's the problem?" Braylin asked again.

"It's just that I'm kind of stuck in this silly dilemma. I have an ex, who's rocking my world right now and has everything that I would love to have in a man." Taylor confided.

"But?" Braylin asked.

"But, he's not Ryan. I think I'm in love with this man, and we've never even gone out on a date." Taylor confessed.

"Ryan? Ryan Smith? He's a great guy. Why haven't you gone out?" Braylin questioned.

"We've both admitted to being interested in one another, but he's my boss… it just wouldn't be right, would it?" Taylor asked, torn in between the two.

"This day and age, the husband is usually the boss, and the wife is an employee. Get with it before you miss out and wind up being even more depressed than you are now." Braylin said, patting Taylor on the back and walking out of the conference room.

Taylor had tried so hard to ignore her feelings, but the shit was getting harder, and seeing Ryan didn't make it any easier. The rest of the week seemed to zoom by with Taylor only talking to Will over the phone. It was her last day in the office for the week, and the way she was feeling, it was going to be for a few days next week as well. Taylor was tired. Will had been working her over. Working on her accounts at work, she needed a mini-break. Plus, she could always work from home.

"Knock knock!" Ryan said, as he knocked on Taylor's door and stepped into her office.

"Hey you. It's the end of the day, end of the week, you leaving?" Taylor asked.

"Yeah, I stopped by to let you know that I'm going back behind the scenes. I think I like not getting up early and dressing up. I like wearing a pair of Jordan's, some jeans, and a nice shirt at home, in my office. So, this is my last day here. I'll still participate in your conference calls and team meetings for this account, but that's it." Ryan said.

"Wow, I'll definitely miss seeing you around. Thanks for everything," Taylor said growing weary of not seeing Ryan again.

Ryan nodded and walked out of Taylor's office, leaving her feeling even more down than she had before. She grabbed her things, shut down her computer, and headed home. Her tub was calling her name, and she was going to answer. She was glad Will had flown back to L.A. to give her a breather. As soon as she walked in, she headed straight for the bathroom. Her feet hurt, and she was indeed in need of a hair wash and long, hot shower.

Taylor stepped in under the water and allowed it to beat down on her stressed shoulders. She lathered her body with her pouf that was covered in her favorite bath wash and massaged the suds into her skin. Her hair fell down her back as the water washed over it. She rubbed her shampoo through her hair and washed it a few times before adding conditioner then turned off the water. Taylor stepped out and wrapped a towel around her head, dried her body, applied lotion, and put on her robe. As soon as she stepped into her bedroom, her doorbell rang. *Who the hell could this be?*

She walked to the door and looked out of the glass window on the side of the door. She damn near jumped out of her skin when she saw who was on the other side of the door. She snatched the door open with a grin.

"Hey! What are you doing here?" Taylor asked bashfully.

"Since I'm no longer working with you, can we go out now? I came over here to see you. I'm tired of playing this damn game with you Taylor…I want you, and I won't stop until I get a yes from you." Ryan confessed.

Taylor was in awe. The way he came at her turned her on, and she too was tired of playing games. She knew she wanted him, and the whole ordeal just gave her a damn headache.

"Come in. Let's talk." Taylor said with a grin.

The both of them sat down on her couch and stared into each other's eyes before speaking.

"How did you know where I lived? This is the second time you've come here." Taylor asked, straying from the matter at hand.

"You work for me. It's not hard to get. I want you, Tay, and I need to know if you'll let me have you." Ryan asked, fed up with the back and forth.

"I..I.." Taylor started, but was quickly cut off by Ryan sticking his tongue into her mouth, sucking her top, then bottom lip.

She kissed Ryan back, climbing into his lap, allowing him to pull off her robe. Ryan kissed and gently sucked on her shoulder, then down onto her breast, pulling her nipple into his mouth. Taylor rubbed her hands through Ryan's hair, then reached down to free his hard dick from his pants. She was shocked that Ryan was packing more than a lot of money in his pants. She grinned before sliding down on his dick and wrapping her hands around Ryan's hands that cupped her breast. She bounced on his dick like a horseback rider.

"Damn Tay, mm." Ryan moaned, biting down on his bottom lip.

"Ooh Ryan, it feels so good." Taylor moaned.

She rode Ryan until he couldn't take anymore. He lifted her up, laid her down on the couch, and made love to her. He propped her leg on his shoulder, then kissed it. Ryan lifted Taylor up and wrapped her legs around his head as he sucked and licked on her sweetness while holding her in the air. Taylor threw her head back and held onto Ryan's head for balance as he licked her into a damn coma. His mouth was the best she'd ever had, and she couldn't take it.

"Gawd! I'm cumming, ooh!" Taylor screamed.

Her juices came out in a gush, quenching Ryan's thirst. He slid her down against the wall on his dick, keeping her legs over his arms. He pounded her into the wall with force. Taylor couldn't do anything but use her muscles to control the force Ryan gave her.

"Shit! Damn baby, you're the best!" Ryan exclaimed.

He let her legs down and bent her over on the wall, then slid back into her. Taylor held onto the wall for dear life as Ryan continued to thrust into her, giving her a euphoric orgasm. Ryan smacked her ass, then bent over to kiss her cheek.

"Damn, baby, I'm about to cum." Ryan belted, before pulling out and releasing himself on her ass.

Ryan walked to the kitchen and grabbed a paper towel to wipe Taylor off then followed her into the bathroom to shower. Once they were done with the shower, Taylor threw on her underwear and a sleep shirt. Ryan pulled on his boxers and the shirt he wore and allowed Taylor to lead him to the bed.

"So what does this mean for us?" Taylor asked.

"Oh, this means you're my woman now, sorry. You're mine." Ryan joked.

"I'm serious." Taylor said laughing.

"I am as well. I want you to be my lady, Taylor Is that alright with you? I don't see why we can't date exclusively and be a couple. I mean, you did say you felt the same way about me. Let's stop wasting time and playing games. We're both adults, and I deserve a shot." Ryan said in a serious tone.

"Okay. Let's do it. We'll see how it goes. So you're my man now… I think I like the sound of that."

Ryan's gorgeous blue eyes sparkled. His smile was gleaming, and the way he flexed his dimples made Taylor giddy like a school girl. He wrapped her up in his arms and kissed her forehead. They held each other until they fell asleep. Taylor knew this was the beginning of a good thing.

Even though it was only about six in the evening when they passed out, they didn't wake up until the next morning. Taylor got up and made omelets with fresh fruit on the side and tall glasses of orange juice to go with it. She spotted Ryan walking downstairs with his shirt off showing off his six pack and muscles. He walked up behind her and kissed her neck, then grabbed the plate she handed him after planting a juicy kiss on his sexy lips. They sat down on the counter stools and ate while glancing at one another.

It was like they had fallen in love after last night. The way they handled each other, the looks they gave. It was at that time that Taylor knew she had made the right decision. She felt relieved. Hell, she didn't even fret when she thought about the fact that she had slept with Ryan unprotected. She knew he was the one for her, and there were no questions in her mind. Her phone sounded off, letting her know she had a text message. Ryan jumped up and grabbed her phone and brought it to her. Taylor gave him a look before taking the phone from him and reading the message.

Will: I've made it home. I had a great time with you this week. Maybe, I should move back…

She tossed the phone onto the counter and continued to eat her breakfast. Just like that, her interest in Sko had depleted and she was looking forward to starting a future with Ryan. Taylor could tell Ryan was curious about the text she'd received, but like a real man, he continued eating, making the moment at hand the most important thing.

"Last night was amazing, and I wanna take you somewhere. Since you're planning on not coming to work for a few days, I want to help you to relax. You deserve it after all of your great work." Ryan said with a grin.

"Where exactly are you trying to take me?" Taylor questioned with a lifted brow.

"I have a cabin out on the lake. It's a modern version of the traditional cabin house. We'll spend the rest of the weekend enjoying one another, eating, watching movies, whatever you want to do." Ryan confessed.

"That sounds great. I'd love that… when do we leave?" Taylor asked hastily.

"We can leave today if you want. I'll make a few calls, and we can swing by my place so that I can pick up a few things and some clothes, and then we can be on our way."

They did just as Ryan said and headed out after packing up a weekend bag. On the way up to the lake, Janae called to hang out with Taylor.

"Hey chick, what's up? You trying to hang today. Jason's giving me a little free time, and I'm bored." Janae exclaimed.

"Ryan and I are headed up to the lake for the weekend." Taylor said.

"Ryan? Oh, okay. You've finally gotten your act together? Damn, my girl getting her rocks off. No more drought for you." Janae chuckled.

"Haha, shut up. I'll talk to you in a few days, hooker, and tell Jason I said hi." Taylor replied.

Ryan smirked at Taylor and thought about how long it took to make it to this point. He was relieved. Now, it was his mission to show her why she made the right decision and to keep her happy. He knew that, once Jason found out about he and Taylor finally trying this thing out, he'd be proud of him. Jason had really been pushing Ryan to not give up, "she could be the future Mrs. Smith," he'd say, and Ryan didn't want to miss that chance. His phone vibrated indicating a text message as he pulled up to the lake house.

Unknown: He's gone back to L.A., and he won't be back for a while. His business has him really busy at this time, and he's going to be flying to New York in a few days, so you don't have anything to worry about.

Ryan slid his phone into his pocket, hopped out of the 2016 Porsche Cayenne, and walked over to let Taylor out of the truck. He watched her hips sway as she walked towards the house.

This is going to be a great weekend.

*****

Janae was in shock, Taylor was changing right before her eyes. First, she let her guard down with Will, and now, she was finally going after the man she really wanted. She was happy for her. Janae knew Taylor had a tendency of not thinking realistically about things. She was a damn overachiever, so you could only expect her to want a perfect relationship. Ever since that damn "relationship" with

Professor Liam, which was a disaster. It had made her tough, somewhat callous to love for a while.

"Baby, your friend finally convinced Taylor to stop acting stuck up. They're on the way to the lake house. Can you believe this shit?" Taylor laughed.

"I taught him well. Let him hang out in the hood with me a few times and now he's running game like a playa," Jason joked.

Janae laughed, "Shut up. You're silly you know. But you did run some hardcore playa shit on me."

Jason laughed wrapping his arms around Janae, kissing her neck. Although they had only been dating for a few weeks, the two had hit it off and were doing great. Janae could see herself being with Jason for the long haul early. She loved the way he treated her. It had been a long while since she'd had a real man. Just like when she was a teenaged girl, Janae loved thugs. It was just something about them. Once she was old enough to realize they meant her no good, she gave them up. See, the thing about Jason was that he used to be a thug, but he was reformed. He was fine, he was successful, and he knew how to treat his woman. She had finally struck gold.

"I got something hardcore for you right here. You want it?" Jason asked grabbing his package.

"Humph, yeah I want that daddy. Meet me in the bedroom," Janae said switching off.

*****

"So, do you like it?" Ryan asked.

"Yes, I love it baby. It's beautiful out here, and this house is amazing. I suppose you just keep food stocked in an empty house?" Taylor asked slyly.

"I admit, I had the housekeeper pick up the food. She lives close by, so she maintains the house and the land, along with her husband."

Taylor smiled. She knew Ryan had a tendency to show out and she loved it. She'd never had a man to really do anything special like take her on a weekend trip. It was the perfect gesture to help her relax and keep her mind off of work. The first night was spent cuddling up, watching movies, and eating in front of the fireplace. Taylor had never seen something so beautiful. The view at the lake house was gorgeous, and at night, the lake would sparkle under the moonlight. She sat on the front porch wrapped in a blanket, admiring the view. Ryan came out and cuddled up with her.

"I could stay here forever. It's so peaceful and so serene. Thank you for bringing me here. I really needed this." Taylor said.

Ryan grabbed her face, kissed her lips gently, then slowly undressed Taylor on the porch. He laid the blanket on the porch and laid Taylor back on it, propping her legs on his shoulders. He gently sucked on her pearl, making it stand at attention and tight center leak with aromatic juiciness. His fingers slipped into her as he lapped and sucked her sweetness, until she reached a climax that echoed through the woods that surrounded them. They made love under the moonlight until they were weak, with just enough strength to make it back into the house to go to sleep.

The next day, Taylor was treated to a boat ride and a delicious seafood meal, courtesy of Ryan. He was fine, and he could cook. He reminded her of someone she once knew. The last night Taylor and Ryan spent as much time together as possible. She felt like letting the people at work know wasn't a good idea.

"In a couple of weeks, my family is having a dinner. It's my mother's birthday, and I'd really love for you to come and meet my family." Ryan said with a grin.

"Um, don't you think it's a little early to be meeting family. It hasn't even been a week since we've been official?" Taylor asked.

"I just want us to let things flow. Let's not hold this up with timelines and restraints. So will you come?" Ryan asked again with a little aggression.

Taylor laughed at his question before responding, yes. Now, she had to worry about his family liking her and what if they're against interracial couples. She couldn't help stressing about every little thing. She was still nervous about their relationship and it getting back to the office. They sealed their deal with some rough sex and a little bit of lovemaking.

*****

Taylor felt like the weekend had gone by too fast. She wasn't ready to go back to work, but she knew with such a large account under her belt, she had to work extra hard to keep it. She was on her way to work when her sister, Trinity, called to check up on her. She didn't even give Taylor a chance to say anything before she was laying into her.

"Damn baby sis. Did you forget about Friday night dinner? Since when do we break tradition? You better have a damn good excuse," Trinity fussed.

"Hello to you, too. Yes, I have a damn good excuse. My man took me on a weekend getaway at his lake house." Taylor gushed.

"Lake House? It's a white boy?" Trinity yelled into the phone.

"Really Trinity? Yes, he's white, but I really like him." Taylor said with a pout.

"I'm going to call mama and tell her about this. We need to meet this clown. Anyway, last I heard, you were back messing with Sko. What happened with that?" Trinity pried.

"Nothing, Ryan just swooped in and took me from Sko. I'm not mad at him. We had a great weekend." Taylor said.

Taylor dismissed Trinity from the phone and walked into her office, noticing Lily giving her this crazy look, before rolling her eyes and looking away. She had always been nice to Taylor, so Taylor chalked it up as Lily having a bad day and kept it moving. Taylor sashayed to her office and was damn near knocked over as Alli ran up on her, pushing her way into Taylor's office.

"Damn! Good morning young man. How may I help you?" Taylor joked with Alli.

"Haha, bitch, I need the details immediately!" Alli exclaimed.

Taylor thought it was odd since she hadn't told anyone but her sister about the weekend getaway with Ryan. Taylor decided to play the role to see what had been said while she was away. Unless Ryan said something to someone, she didn't know how Alli knew that. She just had a weird feeling the second she walked into the building. It's like she knew everyone would just think she'd been gone with Ryan for the weekend.

"I don't know what you're talking about Alli." Taylor lied.

"Look the whole office knows you and Ryan went away for the weekend to his lake house. You know damn well anything Lily knows she's telling any and everybody." Alli confessed.

Taylor instantly got pissed off. This is exactly what she was trying to avoid.

*****

Ryan was laying back in a lawn chair next to his pool, tanning, when suddenly the sun was blocked by something or someone. He looked up and spotted Todd standing over him. He didn't know what was going on, but he didn't want any parts of it by the way Todd was looking.

"Wassup, Todd! Is everything alright at the office?" Ryan asked.

"Yes, everything is good. I'm just curious, why didn't I know about you and Taylor messing around? I thought we were best friends?" Todd asked.

"We are; it just happened, and I didn't have a chance to tell you since we spent the weekend together. How did you find out?" Ryan questioned.

"Someone at the office told me. Anyway, why did you wait until now to talk to her? If this shit takes a left, it may affect her work, which would cause us to lose this account." Todd fussed.

"I didn't look at it that way. I think it affected us both more trying to act like there was nothing there. The attraction is undeniable, and when we're together, we're good." Ryan said.

"Look, you just be careful with her. I don't want you hurting her and ruining things. She's a good girl and a hard worker. Please don't allow this to interfere with work. I suggest ending it before this goes any further." Todd said before walking off.

Ryan sat up in his chair and placed his arms on knees with a defeated look. He couldn't believe his best friend wanted him to end something he tried so hard to get. Todd nor anyone else could stop Ryan from being with Taylor. He cared about the girl and Todd would just need to accept it. Now, the real question was, who the hell was telling their business when he'd only told Lily to have her find out information on Will. He didn't think she would say something. Especially, when he told her not to. Ryan jumped up and ran into the house. He picked up his phone and called Lily.

"Hey, can you meet me on your lunch break?" Ryan asked.

"Sure! Where would you like to meet?" Lily asked.

"Meet me at the café," Ryan replied.

He hung up and pulled on a pair of jeans, a fitted t-shirt, and some Nike shoes. Ryan grabbed his wallet, phone, and keys, then headed out of the door. He had to get to the bottom of this. He hated an untrustworthy person, and Lily was proving to be just that. She was throwing a monkey wrench in everything. Maybe Todd put her up to it. Ryan got to the café, grabbed a table in the back, and told the waiter to bring Lily back to where he was. Shortly after, Lily switched into the café wearing a dress that hugged her curves, and for the first time, demanded Ryan's attention. He gladly gave it. He stood up while Lily was seated at the table.

"Thanks for meeting me at such short notice. I just wanna tell you, you look great, damn! Anyway, back to the matter at hand…" Ryan's voice trailed off.

Lily was sitting at attention like a little puppy, and it had finally hit her, the reason why she let the cat out of the bag.

"I was trying to figure out how the hell the office knew about Taylor and me? Did you say something?" Ryan asked sternly.

"Yes, I did. I'm in love with you and have been for years. Ever since I first started working for you. Then, she comes in and you're smitten? You need to leave that inexperienced girl alone and get with a real woman." Lily confessed, slightly catching Ryan off guard.

"Look, that's nice to hear and all, but you don't have the right to tell me what I need to do. I NEED to stop fucking with you. You can't be trusted. Thanks for your help, but I'm not interested." Ryan said before getting up and walking out of the café.

Lily hadn't expected for her slip of the lip to backfire the way it did. She had been crushing on him ever since she was hired. She remembered it just like it was yesterday. She spotted him walking into the office with his shirt unbuttoned at the top, his sleeves were rolled up, and he had on slim fit slacks with some expensive shoes. Ryan was one of those guys that were so fine; he demanded the attention of everyone in the room. Women loved him, gay men wanted him, and straight men wanted to be like him. His body was sick; he had an eight-pack, with muscular arms and legs and a nice ass. Unfortunately for Lily, she was the furthest thing from Ryan's mind, so she had to settle for Todd, who was trying his best to be seen by her.

Lily got up from the table and left the café with tears streaming down her face. She didn't care what it took; she was going to get her man, and he was going to recognize her for the good woman she was. She sat in her 2015 BMW for a few minutes, trying to get her head straight, then she picked up her phone and called Todd.

"Yes, he said he won't stop seeing her; he loves her. You're not going to get a chance to…" Lily said before she was cut off from a shouting Todd on the other end.

She pulled off with laughter. She had put her plan into motion already. Lily was determined and she wasn't going to stop until she had exactly what she wanted.

Chapter Six

Friday had rolled around again, and Taylor couldn't wait to get home so that she could see Ryan. The past couple weeks had been great. Ryan was proving to be a better fit for her life, and for what she was looking for in a partner. It was the weekend of Ryan's mother's birthday dinner, but for now, she had to meet with her mother and sisters for their weekly weekend dinner. Taylor had made it to her mother's house with her famous taco salad, since they were having a Mexican themed dinner this week. She walked into a table filled with different cooked meats, taco shells, veggies, and condiments for tacos. She added her bowl of taco salad next to her sister's famous Spanish rice.

"Well, look what the cat drug in." Teagan said, watching Taylor switch into the kitchen.

"Yes, the cat drug in this sexy one right here," Taylor said pointing at herself and laughing.

Teagan laughed at her and smacked Taylor on the butt.

"Alright, don't make me whoop you now. Why are you in such a good mood?" Teagan asked.

"I'll tell you later when we all sit down to talk. Now, go over there and make me a plate. Get yourself ready for this when you're married." Taylor laughed.

Trinity and Thandi walked into the kitchen and made their plates, making small talk before they all retreated into the dining room. They sat down for a while enjoying their food before they finally decided to speak.

"So, ladies, I really enjoyed my trip with my honey bun. I know you all saw the pix. Oh yeah, I have souvenirs for you all as well. What's been going on with y'all?" Thandi asked.

"Nothing much, Ma. I'm trying to get used to this whole pregnancy thing. It's kicking my butt. Remind me to never do this again after this one." Trinity said, rubbing her belly.

"Dorian said he wants to come to one of our weekly family dinners, so I think next week we should make it a co-ed dinner this one time. What do you guys think?" Teagan asked.

"I think that would be great, because I really want you guys to meet my baby Ryan. You guys are going to love him." Taylor said, smiling like a Cheshire cat.

"Ryan, huh? What happened to my baby Will? You've dropped him already?" Thandi asked.

"Ma, you only like Will because you know his mama. We were only dating. It wasn't official, but Ryan and I are official. I'm meeting his family tomorrow at his mother's birthday dinner." Taylor exclaimed.

They were excited for Taylor. She had never seemed so excited about a guy she was dating, and it about damn time she had someone she could bring to meet the family. The dinner setting and menu was planned while they listened to music, drank, and laughed. Trinity sat by idly, wishing she could have a drink. She vowed she was going to have a shot of Patron as soon as she came from the hospital, after having her baby.

*****

Taylor was nervous as hell as she scrambled through her closet looking for something to wear. She had a ton of clothes, but for some reason, she couldn't find anything to wear. She knew her nerves were getting the best of her, so she sat down with a glass of wine to relax and think. Taylor finally settled on this silver Dior dress. It was form fitting, yet elegant. She had the perfect pair of Giuseppe's and a clutch to match. She stepped into the dress and was quickly zipped up by Ryan, who had walked in after waiting more than an hour for her to get ready.

"Are you sure this is the one? I've zipped you up twice already." Ryan laughed. Taylor gave him the stink eye.

She looked amazing, and Ryan couldn't keep his eyes off of her. He stood behind her in the mirror, staring at the two of them next to each other. He interlocked his fingers with hers then brought her hand up to his mouth to kiss it. It was exactly how he had imagined they'd look like together. Taylor's long natural hair was silk pressed bone straight with a middle part that accentuated her face. Her makeup was flawless and her light honey brown eyes shimmered in the mirror.

"God babe, you're so beautiful. I sure know how to pick them." Ryan joked.

Taylor laughed, "No, I chose you… and I must say, I have great taste."

They both added their finishing touches, before walking downstairs to enter Ryan's car. They rode to his parents' house, taking their time to allow Taylor to grill him for much-needed information. Taylor hated to go to a meeting unprepared at work, and this was no different. She liked to be on top of her game at all times.

"So, who's going to be there again?" Taylor asked.

"My parents, of course. My sisters, Emily and Leah, and my two brothers, Matt and Steven Jr." Ryan replied.

"Okay. Give me a quick summary of everyone's personality and behavior." Taylor asked, as if she was using a mental notepad to copy down the information.

"My parents, Steven and Janie, are both from wealthy families. They were born with money. My dad has his own law firm and is very successful. My mother has her own catering company, and she has a company that delivers groceries. My sister, Emily, is a joy to be around. She's always nice and polite. She's beautiful inside and out. She's twenty-one, just graduated from MIT, and she's extremely smart. Leah…she's always mean and rude. She's only beautiful on the outside. She can be evil if you allow her. Trust me, she gets a kick out of seeing people sweat. She does absolutely nothing but live off of her trust fund, and she has a six-year-old son, my nephew, Evan. Steven Jr. is a cardiologist/surgeon. He and my brother Matt are like Emily. They're beautiful people to be around. Always helping out and being polite. Matt is a financial advisor. They're both married. Is that enough info?" Ryan said with a smirk.

"Yes, smart ass. By the way, which hospital does your brother work in. My sister is also a cardiologist." Taylor laughed.

"Oh, he works at Emory." Ryan replied.

"Wow! So does Trinity, small world. So that means they work in the same office. Cool!" Taylor said with a grin.

They pulled up in from of his parent's home, which was a huge mansion with a circle driveway. The landscaping was amazing. As soon as they stepped out of the car, they were greeted by one of the butlers. He walked them into the foyer and into the living room where everyone was seated until dinner was served. There were about twenty people sitting there who looked up at Taylor as she walked in. She was glad to see that she wasn't the only black girl in the room. It seems Ryan's brothers had the same thing in mind. Beautiful little biracial children ran around laughing and playing, warming Taylor's heart and allowing her to sigh a bit.

"My baby. I'm so glad you could make it." Ryan's mother, Cristina, said.

"Oh good, mom's favorite kid is here." Leah snapped.

Taylor looked over at her and instantly knew that she was Leah. She gave a fake smile then turned back to Cristina, who was cheesing at Taylor.

"Hey Ma. Happy birthday!" Ryan said, kissing Cristina's cheek and handing her a bag.

Taylor couldn't understand what any of them could possibly need or want as a gift with all of the money they had. She sat down next to Ryan and began talking to Emily and Asha, Steven's wife. Asha looked like a model. She was about 5'9, and she had a reddish brown skin tone, showing off her Native American heritage. Her hair was long and bone straight. She had a deep dimple in her left cheek and had a great body. Just from the conversations they had, you could tell she was smart and independent.

"Taylor, it's so great to finally meet you. Ryan has been going on and on about you for the past two weeks. You have my brother-in-law in his feelings." Asha laughed.

"Oh wow, nice to meet you as well. You are so beautiful. I feel like I can't stop staring at you." Taylor said with a grin.

"I think we all were thinking the same thing about you. You and my brother look great together, and he seems so happy. It's a little early. What did you do to him to make him want to bring you to meet Hell-Leah?" Emily asked with a chuckle.

"Thank you. I really like Ryan. I don't know. We just seem to hit it off instantly, and it just went from there. And he's told me about Leah, somewhat. I hope we can get along." Taylor confessed.

"Don't be surprised if it doesn't happen. She and I actually came to blows before, over a year ago. She really didn't want Steven and me to get married, but she got over it after I beat her ass." Asha smiled, making Emily laugh.

"Dinner is ready for you all. Please follow me." The butler said, leading everyone to the large dining room. The table looked like something out of a movie; it was long enough to seat about forty people.

All of the kids and their spouses were seated near Cristina and Steven Sr.. The remaining family members and friends filled in the rest of the seats. The serving team brought out the salad, followed by the soup. Everyone was indulging in the delicious meal in front of them and small conversations with the people nearest to them.

"So Taylor, where did my brother meet you?" Leah asked.

"I work for Ryan. I'm a marketing manager." Taylor said proudly.

"Oh really? How did you come into that position?" Leah asked, clearly trying to be nasty.

"Well, Todd hired me about a year ago as a marketing consultant, and I just recently became a marketing manager after I landed the largest account in Kragin & Smith history." Taylor said in an unbothered tone.

"That's good, that's good. So you actually went to school for marketing?" Leah asked, trying to get as much information as she could.

"Damn Leah, are you going to ask her twenty-one questions. Eat your food and shut up!" Ryan exclaimed, getting irritated.

"Oh no, baby, it's okay. Leah wants to know more about me. I'd be happy to oblige. I have a Bachelors in Marketing from Spelman and a Master's in Finance from Emory." Taylor said with a lifted brow.

"Okay…" Leah said before Taylor cut her off.

"No, I'm not with Ryan for money. I have my own. I'm debt free, have perfect credit, no kids, no baby daddies. I'm a hard-worker, and I plan on being with Ryan for the long haul. Is that okay with you?" Taylor said with a snap of her neck, making Cristina laugh and turn her head back towards her plate when Leah looked up at her.

"Yes, I am okay with that." Leah said, not saying much more for the remainder of the night.

After dinner, Cristina opened gifts and the guest sipped coffee with the cake before leaving. Ryan and Taylor stayed behind with the rest of his siblings to get some more one-on-one time with their parents. Ryan's father hadn't said much that night, but once everyone was gone, he sat next to Taylor and grabbed her hand.

"This is the first time I'd ever seen my son genuinely happy. Being from a wealthy family and having a successful multi-million dollar company draws a lot of attention from the wrong types of women. When Ryan told me that you were the one to land that Braylin Lee account, and that he had practically gotten down on his knees and begged for you to allow him to take you out, even with you knowing about his status, I knew that you would be a great match for him. Watching you hold your own with my Leah and seeing how beautiful you are with my own eyes has me rooting for you. Don't let me down." Steven Sr. said, patting Taylor's hand and getting up to walk upstairs to his room.

"I agree with my husband. I look forward to spending more time with you Taylor. Again, it was great meeting you. Have a good night." Cristina said retreating to her room as well.

"Brother, it was good seeing you. Don't forget we're meeting up tomorrow to have a guy's night so that we can talk about everything that happened tonight without women breathing down our necks," Matt said dodging a hit from his wife Cami.

Cami, short for Camille was Matt's wife. She was a plus-sized beauty. She was 5'6 and looked to be around 200 lbs., with a tiny waist, and small love handles on her stomach. She was light-skinned with long, skinny blonde dreads that fit her face perfectly. She had a smile that would draw anyone in, and she dressed like she lived on the runway. She was really quiet, only speaking when she really had something to say. Taylor instantly took a liking to Emily, Asha, and Cami. They were people she could see herself befriending. The whole time, Leah was rolling her eyes and giving Taylor a crazy look.

"Well, I gotta get my baby out of here, so I can get some." Ryan joked, making Taylor blush and turn red with laughter.

The couple said their goodbyes and walked out to the car. Ryan pulled off and Taylor started in on the events of the night.

"Everyone was great, except Leah. She doesn't like me, and I'm not too fond of her either." Taylor confessed without hesitation.

Ryan laughed before speaking, "I don't like her ass either. We've never gotten along. She's the second eldest after Stevie. Then, it's Matt, me, and then Emily. Leah has never gotten along with the three of us. Although she and Stevie are extremely close, she just has this "I run shit" attitude towards everyone and everything. The funny part is, she's the only one that didn't go to college. She got her high school diploma and remained a slut from that point on. She got pregnant by one of Steven's friends, who was married, and had my nephew seven years ago. She's trouble, Tay. Avoid her at all costs. You'll only wind up beating her ass like Asha did, and you see how sweet Asha is." Ryan said seriously.

After driving for forty-five minutes, they finally pulled up to Ryan's house. He hurried out of the car and walked over to Taylor's side of the car, opening the door and reaching out for her hand to help her out of the car. Taylor smiled, grabbed his hand, and stepped out of the car. Ryan shut it behind her and walked her in. In his room, they ripped their clothes off and Ryan pushed Taylor onto the bed.

Ryan lifted Taylor's legs and dove into her pussy head first. He licked her from front to back, making her legs twerk like a stripper. Ryan sucked on her pearl gently, making her scream and moan. He used his fingers to find her g-spot, making her cry out with pleasure as he continued to taste her sweetness.

"God Ry, I'm cumming!" Taylor exclaimed.

Once she had emptied her juice box, she pushed Ryan back on the bed and took him into her mouth, sucking down to the base. Ryan had about nine-and-a-half inches of prime beef. Taylor had never seen a white guy with that much to offer, not even on the porn sites she watched when she was horny. She worked her mouth on his muscle, forcing Ryan to grab Taylor by the back of the head and guide her mouth on his dick, while he threw his head back, moaning and biting on his bottom lip.

Taylor was enjoying every stroke Ryan was throwing at her. She stroked and sucked Ryan until his eyes rolled into the back of his head and he pumped faster into her mouth. His thrusts became deeper and stronger.

"Shit, I'm cumming! Ugh!" Ryan yelled before exploding in Taylor's mouth.

Taylor swallowed every drop of love juice Ryan spilled and laid back onto the bed. Ryan kissed all over her body, allowing himself to rise again. He slid into her with force, causing her to moan aloud. Ryan nibbled on Taylor's shoulder and kissed her lips so passionately, he almost felt like he was in love, but he didn't want to cross that line just yet. He had to be sure about her. Ryan sucked on her bottom lip, rubbing his fingers through her hair, making love to not only her body but her mind.

"You're so beautiful. Your sex is addictive. I can't get enough of you baby," Ryan confessed.

He stroked Taylor more, sucking a passion mark on her neck. Ryan pulled Taylor onto his lap, forcing her to ride him and take all of the inches he was serving up. Taylor rode him like a pro, arching her back with every stroke, driving Ryan crazy.

"Oh god, I'm about to cum," Ryan shouted.

He exploded deep within her with a whimper. Taylor passed out, and right after Ryan was done, he followed suit. She knew she was in love with Ryan already, but she couldn't tell him just yet. She needed to fill him out first. Ryan was nothing like Will, but she loved it. Being out of a relationship for so long had Taylor scared witless, but she had to do it if she was ever going to succeed at achieving happiness.

The next morning, Taylor's phone rang waking her up from her deep slumber. Ryan had her sleeping like a baby the way he put it down on her the night before. She kinda hoped he would've answered it for her, but thought about how Sko had been calling her lately. She knew it couldn't be work related on a damn Sunday.

"Hello?" Taylor answered groggily.

"Hey chick! I've missed you. Did you forget you had a best friend? What's up?" Janae asked.

"Hey girl! I was knocked the fuck out. How have you been?" Taylor asked.

"I really need to talk to you. We need to meet up today. Are you going to be free?" Janae asked, sounding like something was bothering her.

"Are you okay? What's going on?" Taylor said, sitting up trying to gather herself.

"I really don't wanna talk about it over the phone. Will you be able to meet me at IHOP? I'm hungry as shit!" Janae exclaimed, making Taylor laugh.

"Yeah, I gotta wake Ryan up to take me home to my car."

"Take you home? You better use one of the many cars he has stashed at his place. And hurry up." Janae fussed before hanging up.

Taylor got up and searched through her drawer of clothes she'd accumulated in the past few weeks from spending the night with Ryan. She found a pair of skinny jeans and a cute cropped sweatshirt. She grabbed a pair of panties and a bra and walked into the bathroom. She turned on the shower and stepped in, letting the water rain down on her face and body. She lathered up and washed off a couple of times before getting out and rubbing on some body butter. She slipped into her underwear, brushed her teeth, and was glad her hair was still straight when she pulled off the shower cap she was wearing over her satin bonnet. She stepped into her jeans, easing them over her curves, then pulled the sweatshirt over her head. She ran a paddle brush through her hair and slid into her flats. By the time she turned to ask about using Ryan's car, he was sitting up in the bed watching her.

"I thought we were past the sneaking out the morning after stage?" Ryan joked.

"I was just about to wake you to ask if I could use your car to go meet up with Janae for breakfast. She needs to talk to me about something. Is that okay?" Taylor asked.

"Of course, baby. You don't have to ask. Which one did you want to take? Just take the Range Rover since the tank is full. Look on that key rack by the door. Now, come here and give daddy a kiss before you leave." Ryan said slyly.

Taylor climbed over to him and kissed Ryan, sucking on his bottom lip then giving him another peck. Taylor climbed off the bed and walked down to the back door. She looked at the key rack and searched through eight different keys before finding the one she needed. She had no clue Ryan owned so many cars. She hit the locks on the remote and climbed into the truck making her way to IHOP. Once Taylor pulled up, she searched the parking lot for Janae's car, finally spotting it not far from the door. She entered the restaurant and was greeted by a waving Janae who was at a table in the back.

"Hey honey, I've missed you so much, boo. We have so much to catch up on," Janae said hugging and kissing Taylor's cheek.

"Well, get me caught up sweetie. What's been going on?" Taylor exclaimed.

"First things first, I have to tell you something...don't judge me either. But...I'm pregnant! I found out a couple of days ago. I'm five weeks, and I'm so excited, but I'm scared to tell Jason. I mean, he may think I'm trying to trap him." Janae said with a pout.

"Trap? Girl, you got your own money and a lot of it; he won't think that, trust me. Just tell him and see what he says. He's a good dude. What else has been going on?" Taylor said.

"Nothing much besides getting myself knocked up. What about you and Ryan?" Janae sang.

"Last night, we went to his mother's birthday dinner. Their house was a huge mansion. His parents seem to like me, and so does his siblings, except his sister, Leah. She was a bitch. Girl, I was ready to put hands on that broad." Taylor confessed.

Janae laughed, grabbing the fork getting ready to dig into the stack of pancakes in front of her. Taylor took a bite of her bacon and sat the rest on her plate before speaking.

"Everything with Ryan just feels so right, but for some reason, I feel like working for him is going to be a problem. Like the first day I went back to work after our weekend getaway, everyone knew we had gone together. I hadn't even told anyone. Somebody at work is telling my business, but I'm going to get to the bottom of this." Taylor said.

"It's probably that ratchet ass friend of yours. You know all she does is run her damn mouth and try to fuck everybody's man. I don't know why you hang with that damn crazy ass white girl." Janae said biting into her sausage.

Taylor stuck a forkful of pancakes in her mouth and started to think of who it really could be snooping in her love life. She hadn't told Alli until after she brought it up to her first, so she knew Alli wasn't the person running her mouth. She continued to eat her food and catch up with Janae for another half hour before they parted ways.

Taylor decided to pop up over Alli's house just to check up on her. She got out of the Rover and rang the doorbell at her condo. After about a minute, Alli opened the door with a robe on. Her hair was pulled back into a ponytail, and unlike every time they'd gone out, she wasn't sporting any make-up; she was natural. Taylor never understood why Alli wore make-up, because she was a natural beauty.

"Hey bitch! What are you doing here? Come in!" Alli exclaimed, pulling Taylor into her home.

"I was out, and I thought about you, so I decided to stop by. I hope I'm not interrupting anything," Taylor said.

"Girl, please! You're always welcome. So how's your boyfriend?" Alli asked with a grin, quickly making Janae's words pop into Taylor's mind.

"We're good, but I've been wanting to ask you something. Do you remember when you asked about our weekend getaway last month? Who told you about that?" Taylor questioned.

"Initially, it was said to be a rumor, but I heard Lily talking about it with one of the other girls from the office. She was saying that you two were sneaking around, and you were cheating on your man with Ryan," Alli confessed.

Taylor sat back and thought about who could have told her about that and the only person she could think of was Ryan. He was the only one who knew about the trip. Hell, she didn't even know until the last minute. She couldn't figure out why Ryan would spread their business in the office, knowing she wanted to keep work and their relationship completely separate.

"Thanks for letting me know. Who have you been doing lately?" Taylor asked with a chuckle.

"I've been messing with this guy named Quan. He's got more meat than a little bit and his money ain't funny. He's sexy, too. I'm getting ready to go see him now." Alli said with a grin.

"Well, I'll let you get to it. I have to go return Ryan's car anyway. I'll call you later." Taylor said, hugging Alli and leaving. Taylor made it back to Ryan's place and unlocked the door with the attached key. Ryan was still in bed watching TV. He had taken a shower and was dressed in nothing but boxers. His body was oiled and his muscles flexed as he stood up to greet Taylor.

"Hey baby. Did you enjoy your breakfast? How's Janae doing?" Ryan asked, kissing Taylor's neck pulling her to the bed to watch TV with him.

"She's good and breakfast was great. I stopped by Alli's house before coming back, and I found out Lily has been running her mouth about me. But you know what I couldn't figure out, was how the hell did Lily know anything about me? We didn't talk, and I didn't tell anyone my business in the office. Alli didn't even know about us going on the trip, but Lily did? Tell me you weren't the one who spread our business in the damn office of all places." Taylor gritted.

"Look, I admit I had her find out some information on Will for me, and I only told her about the trip, because I wanted to make sure Will was out of the way. I didn't know she was going to sneak behind my back and tell everyone our business." Ryan confessed.

"So you were spying on me and my friend? How can I trust you when you're slithering around being sneaky and doing shit behind my back? And let me guess, she likes you? This shit is unbelievable. I'm using your car, and I'm going home. Please don't call me today. You can pick up your car tomorrow." Taylor said storming out and speeding out of the driveway.

Taylor felt betrayed. After finally letting down her guard to allow Ryan to get close to her, he went against everything she's wanted, which was privacy and honesty. She needed to be alone so that she could think about what her next move

104

would be. She made it home and decided a couple bottles of wine and a movie would help her unwind.

Chapter Seven

Drunk and exhausted, Taylor passed out the night before and woke the next day around noon, missing half a day of work. She jumped up and got ready, then headed over to the office. Taylor walked into the office in a black dress, with black shades, no makeup, and her hair pulled into a messy bun. She walked into her office, closing the shades, and locking the door behind her. She sat at her computer with the biggest Caramel Latte with two espresso shots Starbucks could sell her. She sipped as she worked on the accounts she managed. She hadn't even looked at her phone since she'd been awake, but noticed it was vibrating in her purse that she had stashed in her bottom drawer. She pulled it from her purse and saw that Ryan had been calling and texting her all morning. Janae texted her saying that Jason was excited about the baby, and Alli was asking where she was, saying that Todd had been looking for her.

She shot Janae a text congratulating her again and telling her that she was going to call her when she got home from work. They really needed to talk. She was interrupted by Todd knocking on her door and calling her name from the other side. Taylor got up and unlocked the door walking back to her desk without turning back to face him.

"How may I help you sir?" Taylor asked with pure annoyance. She didn't feel like being bothered with anyone face-to-face right about now.

"Are you okay? I noticed that you're just now getting here. You know being a marketing manager, you can stay home sometimes, work from your home office. No one will be mad at you." Todd said, trying to reassure Taylor it was okay to not come in if something was going on.

"Thank you, Todd. I really do need to go home. However, rest assure my work will be done. I just have a lot going on right now. I'll be here bright and early tomorrow." Taylor said, tossing her phone in her purse and closing up the work she was doing on her computer.

She stood up and followed Todd out of her office, walking past him then bumping into Lily.

"Lily, can I talk to you for a second in my office?" Taylor asked, feeling like she needed to get something off of her chest.

Lily followed Taylor back into her office and sat down in the chair that sat directly in front of Taylor's desk. Taylor sat down and crossed her legs and interlocked her fingers in front of her.

"I'm going to say this one time and one time only… please keep my name and Ryan's name out of your mouth if it is not business related. I do not appreciate you talking about us in this office like this is a high school. I will not tolerate you turning my workplace into a messy cesspool for you and your unprofessional co-workers who like to engage in this behavior with you. Know that I'm being a professional woman right now, but if I find that you have tried to come near my man or that you are talking about us in an ill manner, it's going to get real fucking ugly for you. Please don't let this pretty face, degrees, and calm tone fool you. I will put my hands on you. Thanks for the chat." Taylor said, not allowing Lily to get one word in.

Taylor got up and opened the door, allowing Lily to walk out in front of her and back to her desk in front of Todd's office. She continued outside to her car, pulling off and heading home. The day had already been too much for her and she had only been awake for an hour-and-a-half. As soon as she stepped in the door, she went up to her room and changed into a pair of short sweat shorts and a cutoff tank top with no underwear. She laid on her couch with a blanket and watched TV. She didn't have any work left to do, and because she had gotten so much done Friday, she felt like she could afford to fuck off a day or two.

It wasn't long before Ryan was ringing her doorbell and begging to be let in through text messages. Taylor finally gave up the tough act and decided to let Ryan in. She opened the door and sat back down on the couch, pulling her blanket over her.

"So, you're not going to speak to me at all Taylor?" Ryan said, no longer speaking with the hood lingo he had picked up from Jason.

"Ryan, how can I trust you after what you did? What else have you been keeping from me?" Taylor asked.

"I promise I wasn't trying to be sneaky. I was just trying to protect myself, just in case you and Will were really a couple. Yes, I found out about him the night you bumped into him at the bar. I was there, and just before I could come over to speak to you, I saw you leave with him. I asked a few of my people that were in the bar and they told me who he was. I really like you, and I just wanted a chance to allow you to get to know me. We've been good this past month and a half and I really can't see myself not being with you. Will you forgive me?" Ryan pleaded.

Taylor sat quiet for a second, trying to make sense of what he said. She hadn't even spotted him that night, but he did start to come on a little stronger after she and Will had started to rekindle the old flame they once had. And she had to admit, she really liked Ryan and could see them making something out of the time they shared. Taylor grabbed Ryan's hand and pulled him over to her; she had made her decision.

"I will forgive you this time, but no more secrets and no more tricks. I've already checked your little office whore on speaking about our relationship at the office and told her I would have her fired and beat her ass." Taylor said matter of fact.

Ryan starting laughing and kissing Taylor. He shook his head and looked Taylor in her eyes.

"Baby, you're crazy. I promise no more secrets, no more tricks. Let's make this work." Ryan said, laying back on the couch with Taylor to watch TV.

*****

Lily stormed into Todd's office locking the door behind her and plopping down in the chair in front of Todd's desk.

"Can you believe that little whore had the nerve to basically tell me she would have me fired and threatened to beat my ass? Who does she think she is?" Lily questioned.

"Lily she does have the authority to fire you, and I told you it wasn't a good idea to spread that information in the office. Ryan is very private and obviously so is Taylor, so for you to tell that, you basically pointed the finger at yourself. Now, what you can do is figure out a way to get Taylor out of the way. If I can't have her, why should Ryan?" Todd confessed, finally letting the truth be known.

Todd had hired Taylor last year and was instantly attracted to her.

One year ago…

"Thank you, again Mr. Kragin, for hiring me. You will not be disappointed," Taylor said reassuring Todd.

"No problem, Miss Powers. We're all going out for dinner tonight and we'd really love for you to come. What do you say?" Todd asked Taylor, knowing that she wouldn't turn down the offer.

She was a new employee with zero experience being asked to rub elbows with team members of one of the most successful marketing firms in, not only Georgia, but the entire U.S,. She wasn't turning that down for anyone. Taylor went out to dinner with the group and was eventually left alone with Todd. He sat next to Taylor putting his hand on her thigh.

"So, what do say, we leave and go have some real fun? I know a bar not far from here. They serve the best Sex on the Beach." Todd said with a glisten in his eye.

Taylor grabbed Todd's hand and politely sat it down on his lap. "I'm sorry, but I'm not interested. I only came to this dinner to get to know the people I'd be working with a little better. If I have to sleep with you for this job, then I'm going to have to turn down the offer. I came to Kragin & Smith because it's the best company out her. Marketing is what I want to do, and I know I'll be good at it, but I am not willing to compromise my integrity just to do so." Taylor said standing up from the table and getting ready to walk away.

Todd grabbed her arm quickly before she could leave. "I'm sorry, Miss Powers. I did not mean to offend you. I admit, I'm attracted to you and I like what I see, but I do not wish to make you compromise yourself. If you still want it, the job is yours; no stipulations." Todd said with a defeated look.

Taylor walked out, but made sure to be at work early the next day. She wasn't going to let the night before affect her. She had worked too hard to get to where she was.

Present Day...

"Braylin is going to L.A. to start her filming and basically start working from there. Maybe, it would be a good idea to see what she thinks about having Taylor go out there with her for a while to learn about the atmosphere over there and drum up some more outlets for Braylin and new clients for you." Lily said with a grin.

"That's a great idea. I need you to set up a lunch meeting with Braylin, and I'll do the rest." Todd said. Lily got right to work, leaving Todd with a sinister grin on his face.

*****

"Is everything ready? Oh my goodness, I'm so nervous." Taylor said as she helped her sister and her mother prepare everything for the dinner with the men.

"Lil' girl, if you ask me that one more time, I'm going to slap you. Everything is ready; we're just waiting on the men to get here, calm down." Thandi said taking a sip of her wine, causing Teagan and Trinity to laugh like they did when they were younger.

Shortly after, the men began to arrive. Keenan arrived first; he greeted Trinity with a kiss and proceeded to the living room to wait for dinner to begin. Dorian arrived next, making Teagan smile from ear-to-ear. Finally, Ryan had arrived and Taylor couldn't wait for everyone to meet him. She led him to the living room to introduce him to everyone.

"Everyone, this is my sweetie, Ryan," Taylor gushed. She went around the room and introduced everyone by name.

"Damn, this is like the movie, Guess Who's Coming for Dinner?" David, Taylor's stepfather said making everyone laugh.

Ryan had a nervous look on his face, but still laughed with everyone. Thandi welcomed everyone into the dining room where dinner was about to be served. The layout was amazing! There were collard greens, lasagna, pot roast, cornbread, yams, and a bunch of other stuff; it was truly a southern style dinner. Everyone was digging in when Keenan started questioning Ryan about his intentions with Taylor. Keenan had always looked at Taylor as a little sister. He and Trinity had been together for seven years, since Trinity was twenty-two years old and Taylor was just sixteen.

"Mr. Smith, I hear you're one-half of your company and that you all are very successful. With that being said, I know how rich playboys think. They feel like everyone is at their disposal and that they can treat people any way they want...I don't get that from you. Plus, my sister likes you, so you must be a good dude, but I'm keeping my eye on you. If you hurt her, you're going to have a problem on your hands." Keenan said, not missing a bite from his plate.

Ryan took a gulp of his wine and smiled, catching Trinity shooting him a nasty glance. Thandi broke the awkward silence by asking Ryan a few questions about himself.

"Ryan, have you ever dated an African American woman before? Does your family agree with your interracial dating?

And finally, what's in store for you and my baby?" Thandi asked.

"Yes, I've dated black women before. My family loves Taylor for me and they're hoping we work out. They think she's smart, beautiful and will keep me in my place. And I'm hoping this relationship is for the long haul." Ryan confessed, grabbing Taylor's hand and smiling while looking into her eyes.

The group finished dinner, had small conversations over dessert then began to say their goodbyes before leaving. Trinity pulled Taylor to the side to talk to her before she left.

"So what do you think?" Taylor asked.

"He's cool for a white guy, but you'd better be careful. Keenan was right; those playboys don't care about hurting your feelings. You know he really looks familiar; this guy named Jason I know used to hang with a guy that looks like him. Jason was a damn whore and a thug. He was in college, but he still wasn't shit, he did my girl so wrong." Trinity said sounding like she was the one who was hurt.

"Um...Jason is his best friend, and he's different now. He's an attorney now, and he's with Janae, and stop worrying, I know how to take care of myself. I love you sis; see you later." Taylor said, kissing and hugging Trinity then rubbing her belly before walking off.

Taylor got into the car with Ryan and pulled off. They didn't say anything for a while, then finally they both started to speak at the same time.

"So your sister and her husband really have it out for me, huh?" Ryan asked, keeping his eyes on the road.

"No, it's not that. One of her friends dated Jason, and he played her, so now she thinks you're going to do the same with me. She has the whole "birds of a feather" idea in her head. But don't worry about that, we're good together, and that's all that matters." Taylor said, trying to reassure Ryan.

Ryan dropped Taylor off before going home to relax. Once he made it home, he texted Taylor to let her know he had made it, like she'd asked, then hopped in the shower. He got out and wrapped a towel around him then walked into his bedroom to grab underwear. He stepped into his boxers and a pair of pajama pants and walked downstairs to his bar to make him something stiff; he needed a drink to help him unwind after the day he'd had.

He poured a glass of Remy and drank two double shots straight. He sat down on the couch with his third glass and flicked through the channels. Ryan was laughing at some show on TV when he heard what sounded like a door open. He hit the mute button on the remote, then waited for a second before turning the volume back up after not hearing the noise anymore. He was laughing again when he heard bare feet walking across his hardwood floors towards him. Ryan jumped up and turned around to find Lily standing in the living room behind the couch.

"What the hell are you doing here?" Ryan asked, slightly slurring.

"I've missed you. You haven't been in the office, and I really wanted to see you." Lily said with a pout.

"Lily, you really need to leave before Tay finds you here." Ryan said sort of giving Lily a warning.

"I'm not worried about your little girlfriend. I just want one kiss," Lily said, walking over to Ryan and wrapping her arms around him.

She planted a kiss on his lips, then parted them with her tongue, pushing a pill into his mouth with her tongue. Before Ryan realized what was going on, he had already swallowed the pill. Lily continued to kiss Ryan as he weakly tried to push her away. The glasses of alcohol Ryan gulped down left him incoherent and unable to control himself, allowing Lily to take full advantage of Ryan, as the pill he had swallowed started to kick in. Everything started to become a blur. Ryan wasn't sleepy, but he didn't have any control over his body. The last thing he remembered was Lily taking him into her mouth, moaning and making sure to use extra spit to satisfy him. The next thing Ryan remembered was waking up the next morning with a hangover.

What the fuck happened?

*****

"Hi Braylin. I'd like to set up a meeting to go over the sales for the DVD and the recipes and fitness books. The sales have been through the roof with the signings and ads pushing the products out into the public more. Let's get together to go a little deeper. Yes, today is perfect. I'll see you at one." Taylor said before hanging up the phone.

Her marketing ideas pushed Braylin even further into the spotlight, and she wanted to go over new ideas and the plans they already had in play. She prepared her notes and everything she needed for her meeting later. Taylor got up and walked out to the break room to get something to snack on. She had an hour before the meeting and she needed to calm her nerves. This would be her first one on one meeting with Braylin. Taylor got in the break room and was brushed by Lily who was walking out of the break room at the same time with one of her flunkies, one of executives from the first floor, with her.

"Hmm, girl we were going all night long, ooh. He was talking about how his woman didn't know how to satisfy him in the bed." Lily boasted.

"Damn, so you just took this lady's man? You're bold." The other girl laughed.

"I'm going to tag you to this picture on Instagram so you can see how fine my sweetie is and how I put his ass to sleep." Lily said, then walked off.

Taylor had made it back to her office when Alli stormed in telling her she needed to see something on her phone. The photo on the phone caught Taylor off guard, and she couldn't help getting emotional when she laid eyes on a sleeping Ryan who had a naked Lily lying next to him.

"I can't believe this shit. That's why he couldn't wait to take me home last night. That dirty muthafucka." Taylor gritted.

She snatched up her purse and grabbed her things she needed for the meeting. She was going to handle business first then handle Lily and Ryan later. She knew exactly what she needed to do.

*****

Ryan woke up to about ten missed calls and fifteen text messages. He managed to climb out of the bed after twelve in the afternoon. After a few failed attempts earlier, he was finally feeling good enough to stand up straight and keep his eyes open. He showered and got dressed. Ryan prepared himself to return all of the missed calls and texts he'd received, and realized most of them came from Jason. Ryan got worried, so he hurried to call Jason back.

"What's good man? You good?" Ryan asked once Jason picked up.

"Bruh, are you crazy? You cheated on Taylor with Lily and let this bitch post a picture of you two on the Gram?" Jason asked, clearly annoyed.

"What the hell are you talking about?" Ryan asked seriously.

Jason forwarded Ryan a screenshot of the post on Instagram and Ryan damn near dropped his phone when he saw the caption underneath the picture. "My baby and I resting after a night of going in." Ryan wanted to crawl under a rock and die. He couldn't believe that just that quick things with Taylor were already going left.

"Please tell me Taylor doesn't know about this?" Ryan asked Jason nervously.

"She texted Janae that she and you were done, and she was not going to believe the bullshit this time." Jason confessed.

"I don't remember any of this. I know last night I was in the house drinking Remy straight and get messed up, trying to unwind after being grilled by Taylor's family, then I heard footsteps and Lily was here. I do remember the bitch kissing me while I was drunk and putting something in my mouth." Ryan told Jason, remembering bits and pieces of what happened.

He ended the call with Jason, grabbed his keys, and rushed out of the door. He had to speak to Taylor as soon as possible. Ryan called Alli's phone and got her to tell him where Taylor was. He had to tell her what happened. Alli told him about the meeting place she had set up with Braylin and that he had better prayed she wants to hear what he had to say. Ryan pulled up outside of the Brazia restaurant and spotted Taylor in her car reading over papers and going through folders. He go out and tapped on her window. Taylor let down her window and rolled her eyes as she turned to face Ryan.

"What the fuck do you want?" Taylor asked in a snappy tone.

"Baby, I promise you I did not sleep with that girl, and if I did, I don't know how it happened." Ryan said, he then continued to tell Taylor about what he remembered and how he was going to fix everything.

"Look, I told you I wasn't going for the bullshit. I told you it wasn't going to be pretty if I got hurt. Not only did you sleep with this tramp, but you let the hoe post pictures tagging the people from the office knowing that we're together." Taylor cried.

"I swear I would not do that! Think about it. I'm going to sleep with her after I told her to stay away from me, after she's been with Todd, and then allow her to be able to throw something in your face, knowing she would want to after that posting? Hell no! I would never do that. You gotta believe me Tay!" Ryan exclaimed.

"If you'll excuse me, I have work to do. This matter can be discussed at another time. Have a good day." Taylor said, stepping out of the car, brushing past Ryan, and hitting the alarm as she switched over to the restaurant.

Ryan was left standing in the parking lot with a stunned look on his face. He didn't know how to take what Taylor had just said. He was falling in love with her and not being able to speak to her was killing him. Ryan drug his feet back to his car and sat there for a minute wrecking his brain on what he should do. First things first… he needed to find out what the hell happened last night. How did Lily know he was home alone and what he was doing? It was almost like she was watching him. Ryan started his car and sped off heading to his house. He got home and started searching around for cameras in the living room and in his bedroom.

Unable to find anything, Ryan plopped down on his couch; the exact spot he was sitting in when Lily came in and laid his head back on the couch. He turned it to the side to face a picture on the wall. There was something odd about the picture. He got up and walked over to it and spotted a small hole right in the middle of the eye of the person on the picture. Ryan lifted the picture from the wall and spotted the small lens that was impressed into the frame. Ryan snatched the camera out, ran out of the door, and drove over to his friend Logan's house.

Logan was a tech geek and could hack into anything. He'd done some work for Ryan in the past, so Ryan knew Logan would be able to help him. Logan opened the door for Ryan and led him to this back room that had several computers set up. Ryan handed Logan the camera, and he went straight to work.

"I need you to find out what was recorded, if that's possible." Ryan said. Logan nodded his head and took only ten minutes to pull up the video from that night.

The video showed a drunk Ryan stunned by Lily. Lily kissed him, and you could tell Ryan was asking her something. She laughed and started to kiss him more. Lily stripped Ryan down to his underwear and started to suck on him like a leech. Ryan was visibly becoming loose and started to pass out. Lily shook him to wake him up, then walked him upstairs. The video was connected to another camera that was in his room. The angle of the video let Ryan know that the camera was placed on his dresser. On the video, Ryan got into bed and fell asleep. Lily stripped naked, took some photos, and left. Ryan smiled, he knew he hadn't slept with Lily; he couldn't. His dick would not get hard if he wasn't attracted to a woman. No matter how hard she tried to throw it at him.

This was great news for him and horrible news for Lily. She was going to pay for this, but Ryan just had to get his lady back first.

Chapter Eight

It had been about two weeks since that shit happened with Ryan and Taylor was still pissed. Every time he called her, she sent him straight to voicemail. Taylor felt like it was nothing to say when her eyes had seen what the truth really was. Will was back in town, and she knew he would definitely help with getting her mind off of Ryan. He was coming over to Netflix and chill, and she wasn't planning on watching a movie.

Taylor opened the door and allowed Will to walk in and hug her. His cologne permeated the air in the room and instantly made her tingle between her thighs. She nuzzled her face into his chest and thought about how much she'd missed him. Taylor's relationship with Will had always been on a physical level; the time they didn't spend sleeping together was like hanging with a best friend or a brother. It was nothing like what she and Ryan had, but since that relationship was shot to shit, she had to make due.

"Damn sexy, I've missed you. You've been keeping it warm for daddy? Will asked, wrapping his arms around her and bending down to kiss her. Taylor looked so tiny standing next to Will, but his height, his body, and his overall look was what attracted her to him; she felt safe with him. Will had brought a couple of pizzas with him and a bottle of Hennessy. Taylor laughed when she saw him whip out the bottle.

"Oh, you're really trying to get into some shit huh?" She asked Will with a grin.

"You already know it, baby, you're not?" Will replied.

"I definitely am," Taylor replied, turning on a movie on Netflix and licking her lips.

Will leaned over and planted a juicy kiss on Taylor's lips, then pulled her onto his lap. Taylor straddled Will, kissing him from his lips to his neck. She pulled his shirt over his head and exposed Will's tatted and toned chest. She just wanted to lick on his tattoos, so she did. Taylor was still kissing Will's chest when she started coughing and gagging like she was choking.

"You good baby?" Will asked, pushing her back to look at her face.

"Um, Sko…is that my name right there or do you know another Tay?" Taylor asked with her eyes bucked.

"Nah, that's you sweetie. I know we're not together, but I'm really feeling you, and I feel like, once you realize what you want, right here is where you'll end up… with me." Will said with a twinkle in his eye.

He was just so fine. Taylor had a hard time turning him down for anything, but she knew, deep down, that she really wanted to be with Ryan. She just couldn't get over what he had done, so for that, she was going to try her best to move on. Will laid her down on the couch, undressing her, then kissing and sucking on her sweetness like it was a treat. Taylor's head flew back, and every thought in her mind about her and Ryan went right out the window. It was going to be a long night and Ryan had no chance of being in her thoughts with Will having his way with her.

*****

Taylor and Janae were in the mall getting a little retail therapy for Taylor, who was still conflicted by this whole love triangle she was involved in. They were in Macy's looking at dresses when Leah walked straight up to Taylor.

"Hey, how are you? Tasha, right?" Leah asked in a nasty tone.

"No, it's Taylor and how are you?" Taylor asked smugly.

"I'm good, how are you and my brother? He's been a little upset lately, and I heard that you left him. What happened? He wasn't thug enough for you?" Leah asked matter of fact.

Taylor gritted her teeth and clenched her jaws. She wanted to hit Leah so bad, but she knew that she couldn't do that.

"Excuse me? Your brother got caught cheating, so he has to deal with his consequences. And furthermore, I've grown sick of your nasty tone and ignorant behavior. I'm trying to remain a lady and refrain from putting my hands on you, but you have one more time to say one of your slick ass remarks." Taylor gritted.

Janae was wearing a huge grin. When Taylor was mad her tone was different and she was downright ratchet. Taylor may have been a corporate woman, but she was from the hood, and she didn't care when she had to show that side of her. If it was necessary, you were going to get it. Janae rubbed her stomach and stood back, just in case Taylor decided to swing on Leah. Janae was tired of Taylor always trying to justify things and allowing people to get so far with their level of disrespect towards her.

"Ha, am I supposed to be afraid of you and your little ghetto friend? You just stay away from my brother," Leah said, drawing her final straw from Taylor.

Taylor's hand reacted before her mind could. She had punched Leah in the face, making blood squirt from her nose, and causing Leah to fall back onto the floor. Taylor continued to pay for her things and left the store. Janae followed behind her laughing the entire time, until they sat down in Taylor's car and pulled off.

"Damn girl, you knocked that white girl the fuck out!" Janae exclaimed with a burst of laughter. "Hell nah! That bitch was out of line though. Who does she think she is? Ryan is going to be livid when he finds out." Janae continued to laugh.

"Fuck him and her. I'm sick of her shit and his. We haven't even dated long enough to be having these types of issues. Like, who does what he did?" Taylor questioned, keeping her eyes on the road.

Taylor drove over to Janae's house where Jason was waiting. He walked outside to help Janae with her bags. He was acting like she was eight or nine months pregnant, the way he was babying her. She was only four months and barely showing. Taylor still thought it was cute. She thought about what having a baby would be like with Will, then discarded the thought when Ryan popped into her head after Jason's question.

"Damn girl, what the hell have you been doing? You got blood on you? And why are you giving my boy such a hard time? You need to hear him out. Just give him a chance to explain things to you. Look, behind closed doors, he told me that he didn't do it. See, I know the type of guys we were in the past, so I know what he's capable of, but he's never lied about it before, so why start now?" Jason asked.

Taylor shot Jason a stare causing him to look away. He didn't want any parts of the bullshit Taylor was ready to dish. He was trying to help Ryan out, but he needed more to give her. Just saying he didn't do it wasn't enough to stop Taylor from being upset. Jason had never known Ryan to go so hard for one chick, so it must have been something about Taylor. She said her goodbyes to Janae and rolled her eyes as she pulled off.

Taylor pulled up to her house and quickly became irritated. Ryan was there again waiting on her. It was the third time this week and she was sick of it. She drove right into her garage and let the door down behind her. Taylor grabbed her bags from the trunk and walked through the kitchen and upstairs to her bedroom to put her bags in the closet.

"Taylor open this door! I really need to talk to you!" Ryan yelled, causing a scene outside.

Taylor walked downstairs and snatched the door open. Ryan was standing there glaring at Taylor with his evil stare. It wasn't like the other days, when he looked like he was wearing his heart on his sleeve. He looked like he wanted to rip her head.

"What the hell did you do to my sister? She came over my house with a bloody face, saying you had beat her up in the mall," Ryan spat angrily.

"Fuck her! I told her to stay out of my face and to stop talking to me. She kept going until I popped her ass in the face. I bet she learned her lesson." Taylor said with a grin.

Ryan was shocked at how Taylor was acting, and it was clear that she was beyond angry. His face softened and a smirk started to form. He could no longer be angry at her, when he realized how much he had missed her.

"Tay, I really need to you to hear me out… I did not cheat on you with that girl. She set me up, and I have proof," Ryan exclaimed.

"I'm sorry, Ryan, but it's too late. I've moved on." Taylor confessed, knowing her heart was still with Ryan. Although she couldn't say it out loud, she had fallen for him; it was just too late.

Taylor shut the door in Ryan's face and got ready for her night with Will. She showered and put on one of the dresses she bought at the mall and applied her makeup. Will called to let Taylor know that he was pulling into the driveway. Taylor hung up the phone, grabbed her purse and keys, and walked out of the door. She locked the door and turned around to see Ryan sitting in one of the chairs that were situated in the corner on her front porch. Taylor ignored Ryan and kept walking down the stairs towards Will's car, letting Ryan's calls out to her fall on deaf ears. Will got out of the car and walked over to Ryan.

"Excuse me, can I help you bruh?" Will asked stepping towards Ryan.

"I'm just trying to talk to my girl, Tay!" Ryan called out, trying to step around Will.

"Look, she's moved on. What you two had is over. Just leave and don't come back, you got it?" Will said pushing Ryan back and turning to get back in the car.

Ryan pushed Will back and they began to have a scuffle. Taylor got out of the car and got in between the two of them, trying to break them apart. Will swung and hit Ryan in the face, causing him to stumble back. Ryan lunged towards Will, knocking Taylor down, and swung but missed him.

"Stop this shit now! Ryan, you and I are finished. You made your fucking bed, now lie in it! Will let's go now!" Taylor shouted.

They got into the car and sped off. Taylor was furious at the way the two of them were acting, but at the same time, amused to see both of the men she cared about fighting over her. She was going to enjoy being the center of attention, but she knew she had to make a decision and to do it fast before someone got hurt.

*****

Todd called Taylor into his office shortly after the start of the day on Monday morning to have a one-on-one meeting. Taylor walked into his office and sat down in front of his desk, crossing her legs and interlocking her fingers. Todd walked from the door and sat back down at his desk, pulling a folder from the drawer and opened it in front of him.

"Thank you for coming to talk with me today Taylor. And I'm so happy that the meeting with Braylin went well, which brings me to why we're meeting today. After talking with Braylin and discussing her next move, you were brought up. As you know, Braylin will be going to L.A. to start filming her cooking and lifestyle show soon, and because you helped her and her agent secure that opportunity, Braylin would like for you to come out with her to personally handle the marketing for her upcoming products and her new show. You can choose your team to go with you and this opportunity will last for the duration of her taping, which will be for three months. Now, you don't have to make a decision now, but you will need to let us know by the end of next week." Todd said, secretly hoping she'd take the offer.

"Wow! That's awesome!' Taylor said at a loss for words.

"Here's the proposal, new salary information, and the stipulations of this agreement. We will cover the cost for moving, securing your new place, and everything you need to get settled, so you won't have to worry about that. You'll let me know as soon as you've figured it out, correct?" Todd asked, holding out his hand.

"Absolutely! I'll let you know. Thank you Mr. Kragin for this opportunity." Taylor said before getting up, shaking Todd's hand, and leaving his office.

It was like everything was going right. Her and Will were good and now this new job offer. She was going to discuss the new position with her family and with Will to see what they thought about it before making a final decision. Taylor was relaxing in her office after completing her work for the day, and she wanted to tell Alli about the new job, since she would definitely be one of the chosen team members, should she choose to take Todd and Braylin up on their offer. Taylor called Alli in and started to tell her about the new job when Ryan burst into her office.

"Alli, can I talk to Taylor for a minute? Just one minute please." Ryan pleaded.

Alli stepped out so that Ryan could speak with Taylor in private, but not before Taylor could give her an evil stare.

Alli threw up her hands. "What? Damn! That's still my boss you know!" Alli said closing the door behind her.

"What do you want Ryan? How can I help you?" Taylor asked with an attitude.

"I want to show you something. Ryan pulled out his phone and showed Taylor the video from the night of the dinner. He watched her attentively to watch her expression upon viewing the video.

"So you didn't do it, huh? She still sucked your dick, and again, I've moved on. I'm sorry." Taylor said handing Ryan the phone and walking out to the desk where Lily sat.

"Can you step into my office please?" Taylor asked.

Lily walked into the office where Ryan was sitting and turned around with a snap of her neck.

"What's this about?" Lily spat.

Taylor locked the door, snatched Ryan's phone, and handed it to Lily. She watched the video in shock, then straightened her face as she handed the phone back to Ryan.

"What did I tell you I would do if I had any more problems with you?" Taylor asked Lily.

Lily started to laugh, but was quickly stopped by the blows Taylor started to rain on her. She punched Lily in the nose, then in the eye before Ryan was finally able to grab Lily and get the office door open. Taylor grabbed her things and went home for the remainder of the day with Alli chasing behind her. Alli had been in the window the entire time, killing herself laughing.

Taylor didn't want to talk, she just wanted to get home. The entire ride home, she thought about something Braylin said at the one-on-one they'd had.

"Take a vacation from the office, you're too good to be cooped in one place, and you're so damn good at what you do, you can have your own firm. This place is nothing but negativity for you. It's just something about you. When you come around ,I get that feeling that Kragin & Smith is not for you, however, I know that Ryan is. Just make sure to take everything into consideration when you're figuring out your next move."

Taylor didn't know how Braylin knew, but she did feel like she was outgrowing that place. Everything she touched turned into gold and she just needed more opportunities to display her gift. Maybe having her own firm was a good idea. She just needed to talk to someone about this. Taylor drove over to Thandi's house to get some insight. Her mother was extremely business savvy, and she knew how to think logically when it came to handling business. Plus, she knew that her mother would give it to her straight.

"Hey Ma! How are you?" Taylor said, kissing and hugging Thandi, trying to make sure her slightly swollen and bruised fists were hidden.

"Hey baby, sit down. You look like something is troubling you. Tell me what's going on?" Thandi asked.

"Ma, everything is so messed up right now. I just wanna run away and never come back. I found out Ryan was telling the truth about not cheating. I had to beat the hell out of Lily for messing with our relationship, and I was offered a great opportunity, but that means I'd have to move to L.A. I just don't know what to do. I want to forgive Ryan, but I'm having such a great time with Will, so I don't see a point. I'm tired of the drama at my job, but at the same time, I don't want to miss out on this great opportunity."

Thandi took a deep breath and exhaled before speaking. "Do what's best for you? If you're going into that office every day is affecting you, then stop. Take the new job in L.A.. You never know, you may find bigger accounts and be able to work your magic and get contracts with them under your own company. You need to learn how to stop allowing yourself to get so overwhelmed with the things that are going on around you. You know that these are things that are out of your control. You've always done that, just like that situation in college. You were messing around with that damn professor and you winded up getting pregnant. That man was in love with you, and because of what everyone else was saying, you let it affect you to the point of having a miscarriage. He winded up resenting you for that; you didn't even hide the fact that you were excited about losing the baby. It took him leaving you and treating you like dirt for you to realize how much you had lost by focusing so much on success and dismissing love. And instead of learning from that, you're doing it again. Hmph, you're just like your father. I used to sit around thinking he was cheating on me until I found out he was only out working himself like crazy, trying to be the best at everything. The night he died, he had been in the office all day and was too tired to notice the drunk driver swerving in and out of lanes. It was too late." Thandi wept.

Taylor let the tears stream down her face after trying to wipe them away. She was tired of trying to be strong and act like nothing bothered her. She was almost twenty-four years old, and she was stressing life like she was a forty-year-old fuck up. She was successful, and she felt like she was punishing herself anytime she acted like a normal twenty-three-year-old. She had made her decision and she was going to let life guide her. She was no longer going to try to live by an outline when it came to her personal life.

"You're right, Ma. I want to be more than just a hard-working employee at someone else's company. I want my own. The position will take me to L.A. for three months, and I think it'll be a good change for me. Maybe, permanent. I want to be with someone who makes me happy, I'm going to talk to Will and go from there. Thanks, Ma!" Taylor said, kissing Thandi's cheek and heading out of the door.

Taylor hit the speakerphone option on the display in her car and called Alli.

"Hey boo! Are you good, is everything okay?" Alli asked with concern in her voice.

"Yeah, I just needed to get a breather. I was offered an opportunity to go to L.A. with Braylin and run her personal marketing campaign, and I have the ability to choose a small team to go with me... I want you to come, what do you think?" Taylor asked.

"Oh, hell yes! I'm down! Who else are you placing on the team?" Alli asked.

"I'm going to ask Tim. He has connections with so many people in L.A., and he's so damn good at this, I'd be a fool not to offer him the opportunity. I'm thinking about starting my own company…I really need a change Alli, I just hope this is the right decision." Taylor confessed.

"Don't worry sweetie. Everything is going to work out, and I'll be right there with you every step of the way." Alli said. Her tone was different; she wasn't speaking in her ratchet manner, and it was like she knew Taylor needed her to be a woman and a good friend at that moment.

"I'm going to call Tim and see what he says about the offer, I'll call you back Al." Taylor said. She hung up and called Tim next.

Tim was like the male version of Taylor, but with connections to so many celebrities and people who ran large companies. He was cute and quiet and never indulged in the antics that always took place at work. Tim was about 6 feet tall, with a nice body, and light, caramel skin. He had deep dimples and dreads with gorgeous eyes. Taylor could remember thinking about how cute she thought he was when she first started at Kragin & Smith, but Tim wouldn't give any of the women there the time of day. Everyone thought he was gay, but that idea was dumped when someone ran into him out on a date with some girl that worked at the café. Tim was private, and Taylor loved that about him; she admired his ethics.

Tim picked up after a few rings. "Hey Taylor!" He said, clearly recognizing her number.

"Hey Tim. I have a proposition for you…" Taylor sang.

"Oh Lord, what's going on Tay?" Tim asked.

"I was offered an opportunity to go to L.A. for a few months to run the marketing campaign for Braylin, and possibly look into drumming up more business for us...maybe our own company? You have plenty of connections. Hell, you eat, sleep, and breathe this marketing shit, and you're the best, next to me of course. I was told I could select a small team to go with, and I want you and Alli to come. Your thoughts?" Taylor said, almost holding her breath. She knew that if she could snag Tim, she was going to shake things up in L.A.

"Hmm...let me think about it." Tim said, still sounding unsure.

"Okay, let me know when you make your decision." Taylor said, about to hang up the phone, before Tim cut her off.

"Alright, I'm in. If we're talking about starting our own company, then you definitely have me for that. I've talked to you about that months ago when you got your first account. You did that shit so effortlessly. We'd be fools to continue battling people in KRAGIN & SMITH when we know we could do this shit in our sleep, while they have to try hard." Tim said.

Taylor told Tim they'd discuss all of the details later, and she was glad that he had her back on this. This move was getting easier and easier. Everything seemed to just fall into place for her.

Maybe Braylin was right...I hope.

139

Taylor drove over to Will's condo, where he was expecting her. She switched over to his door and lifted her hand to ring the doorbell, but was pulled into a hug by Will. She sat on his couch and enjoyed the glass of wine he poured her. She told him all about what happened at the office and the job offer she had received.

"Damn baby... here you need some more of this." Will said, pouring Taylor another glass of wine. "Now about this move... you already know I'm excited. You're going to be moving to my neck of the woods, but seriously, you really do deserve this, and if this will help you to get your foot in the door for starting your own company, then I support you wholeheartedly. No matter what's going on between us, I want you to be successful. Congratulations, babe!" Will said before wrapping Taylor up in his arms then making love to her right there in the living room.

*****

Ryan sat on the couch drinking a beer and trying to think of something to do. His doorbell rang, and he hopped up to see who it was. It was Jason and Todd, oddly coming to cheer Ryan up together.

"Wassup, bruh! We came to help you get yourself together. Look at you, you need a damn shave. Taylor has you stressing like that? Damn, she must have that bomb kitty." Jason said with a chuckle.

Ryan smiled and nodded his head to agree with what Jason said.

"What are the both of you doing together? I must be out there bad to have brought you two together. Really, I'm good. I finally came to my senses. She's moved on and so will I. I need something to get into, if you know what I mean." Ryan said with a sinister grin, looking at Jason.

"I have the perfect one for you. She's sweet, innocent, and she's sexy as hell!" Todd exclaimed.

"Ah damn, a white girl?" Ryan asked, making Jason laugh.

"Actually, she's mixed, half black/half Spanish. You'd love her. Here's her number. Call her and take her out." Todd said, handing Ryan the number.

"You can't sit over here pouting over Taylor forever. She's with that Will dude now, and she's getting ready to move to L.A. for her new position," Jason said smiling and looking at Todd, as to say 'it's his fault'.

"L.A.? What the hell is in L.A.?" Ryan asked leaning up and setting his beer down on the table.

"Braylin wants her to work with her in L.A. to help drum up more marketing opportunities in that area, so I offered her the position, along with a small crew of people she's comfortable working with. It's only for three months." Todd replied, nervously. He knew Ryan would be mad at him for doing that.

"I can't believe this shit. You're sending her all the way across the country to be closer to the muthafucka that's stolen her from me. Thanks a lot, Todd; a really great friend you are." Ryan said, getting up and storming out of the room.

Jason looked over at Todd who had a defeated look and laughed before turning his head and getting up to check on Ryan. He hated to see Ryan like this, but Jason felt like he needed to suck that shit up and try to get with the girl Todd was hooking him up with.

Ryan stormed into the kitchen, leaning onto it with both arms. He couldn't believe he had another obstacle to climb to try and win Taylor back. It was like God was punishing him for finally falling in love with someone after all of the heartbreaks he had caused in the past. He cleared his throat, stood up straight, then picked up his phone. He wasn't going to let Taylor be the only one having fun and moving on. He dialed the number that Todd had given him and waited for Alana to pick up. She sounded so beautiful. He just hoped her actual appearance matched her voice.

"I'm good y'all, I called Alana, and we're going to meet up tonight, so I need to get ready, bye." Ryan said, pushing them out of the front door. He exhaled and prepared himself for his date.

Once Ryan was dressed, he stood in the mirror and gave himself a pep talk. He had on a pair of jeans, a nice shirt, and a pair of loafers. He was stunning, like a model, as usual. He grabbed the keys to the Lambo and sped off. He wasn't doing anything special to impress Alana. He just decided to drive that car because it matched what he was wearing. He made it to the restaurant Alana chose and got out, handing his keys to the valet attendant. Ryan straightened his clothes, then walked over to the hostess and told her he was meeting someone and that he was to sit at the far table in the back. The girl smiled at Ryan and tried to flirt with him.

"It would be a pleasure to help you, sir. I'll walk you over to that table now." The hostess said, leading Ryan to the table where Alana sat.

"Thank you so much," Alana said to dismiss the girl, who rolled her eyes once she spotted Alana.

Alana stood up, and to Ryan's surprise, she was beautiful. She was built Ford, tough. Her stomach was flat, with a little of her stomach and her navel showing. She had on a dress that made her breast look like two melons, and her ass looked like two basketballs were smuggled underneath her dress. Her pretty honey colored skin looked soft, and Ryan had hoped it tasted as sweet as it looked.

"Hey! I'm Ryan, Alana, right?" Ryan asked trying to introduce himself.

"Yes," She replied, wrapping her arms around him.

Alana and Ryan talked and got to know each other a little better, but it wasn't long before they were heading to a hotel room and kissing each other rough and passionately. Alana pulled off her dress and blew Ryan away with her body. You could tell she was a fitness junky. She had a six pack and her legs looked like a stallion. Ryan knew she was going to try to give him a run for his money. With this beautiful woman standing naked in front of him, he still had thoughts of Taylor in his head... how much more beautiful she was, how good her sex was, and the fact that she was moving away with that guy. Alana started to kiss Ryan bringing him back to the matter at hand. He kissed her back, laying her down on the bed.

Ryan took her breast into his mouth, then kissed down to her navel and back up. He couldn't take it there with Alana. He didn't know her and to him that was something you left for your woman or your wife, and she was neither. Alana flipped him over and went down on Ryan, making his toes pop. He had to look down at her to see it for himself. Alana sucked and slurped on him like a professional, making Ryan secretly hope she wasn't a damn call girl as good as she was doing him at that moment. She took Ryan's dick deep into her mouth without gagging and pulled it out and kissed the tip in admiration. Ryan pulled out the Magnum that he filled so snugly and slid it down on his dick once she was done handling his piece. Alana smiled then slid down on his dick and started bouncing and grinding like she invented the shit. She had Ryan in his feelings and he was in need of that feeling. He wrapped his arms around her and rubbed his fingers through her hair, sucking her right breast at the same time.

"Ooh Ryan, shit!" Alana moaned.

Ryan started to thrust deeper and harder as he began to think about Taylor. She was like a drug, and he couldn't get enough of her. He went harder and deeper.

"God Ryan, ooh damn!" Alana screamed.

When he couldn't hold out anymore, Ryan pumped until his seeds were about to spill into the condom.

"Tay, I'm cumming!" Ryan grunted, before Alana collapsed on his chest.

Alana rolled over watching Ryan get up and walk into the bathroom to get cleaned up. He came back into the room and laid down next to her. She stared into his eyes before speaking.

"I…I guess Tay is the one that got away?" Alana asked.

"How do you know that?" Ryan asked.

"Well, you just called me her name. You know, I have to be honest… when Todd first told me about you and what you'd just went through, I was a little iffy about going on this date. But, I too have just gotten out a relationship and experienced a messy break-up. But it's okay, I'm not blaming you for feeling the way you do. I think about my ex as well. We don't have to make anything serious of this. Let's just have fun and let the chips fall where they may." Alana confessed.

That gave Ryan a sense of comfort. He felt like this was happening too fast. He wasn't afraid to admit that he took this break-up a little hard, but to hear that Alana was going through the same thing made things easier. Ryan wrapped Alana in his arms and kissed her until they fell asleep in each other's arms. *This was just going to be sex and dates until he got his woman back,* was the last thought Ryan had before falling fast asleep.

Chapter Nine

Janae climbed in bed on top of Jason and just watched him sleep for a minute before shaking him to wake him up. She lightly slapped his face and kissed him awake.

"Jay, wake up baby!" Janae yelled with laughter, scaring the hell out of him.

"Yeah baby, you good? Is everything okay?" Jason asked wiping his eyes.

"Yeah, I'm just trying to figure out why you and Todd thought it was okay to hook Ryan up with some tramp. What happened to getting him and Tay back together?" Janae said with a pout.

Jason sat up and wrapped him arms around Janae and kissed her neck. "Baby, she doesn't want him, so we needed to do something to cheer him up…the man needed some pussy." Jason chuckled and tried to kiss Janae.

"Eww, get away, your breath stinks. Go brush your teeth. " Janae exclaimed and ran out of the room as if Jason was chasing her.

Janae busted out in laughter once Jason caught her and kissed her in the mouth. She had led him right to the bathroom to brush his teeth. She stood back and watched him wash up and get himself together, the whole time a smile adorned her face. She was in love, and the moment she told

Jason, he couldn't wait to tell her the same. They fell fast and hard, and with a baby on the way, Janae was hoping it was a permanent thing.

"You good baby?" Jason asked.

"Huh? Yeah, I'm good. I was just thinking about us. We're going to be parents. I just want things to work out with no issues. And I just keep thinking about Tay. That's my best friend, and I want her to be here when I deliver this baby, not off in L.A. somewhere. I want all of us to be able to be in the same room. I know you and Ryan are best friends and you want him to be our baby's godfather, and I want Tay to be the godmother... we gotta fix this." Janae said.

Jason knew it was nothing he could do, and he was tired of focusing so much on Ryan and Tay's problems. He was happy to finally have a family, a woman who loved him for him and not his money. He was raised by his grandmother after his mother was wrongly accused for a crime she didn't commit and was sentenced to fifteen years in jail, when Jason was ten. She had a public defender who didn't know anything about her case or give a damn for that matter. What happened to his mother was the reason why he became an attorney. He wanted to make sure more innocent people weren't convicted of crimes they didn't commit without evidence. Once he was sick of fighting the system being a defense attorney, he went on to become a corporate attorney.

The relationship Jason and his mother has is still a strained one, but he knew it wasn't her fault. He never had a father, and the man his mother was married to was an asshole. She was accused of drugging her ex-husband, trying to kill him, which supposedly caused him to swerve into a lane and kill a man in a wreck. Her ex-husband told the police, he and Jason's mother had been arguing, and after the argument, she brought him a glass of juice that made him feel funny. By the time he got down the road, he was feeling woozy and that's when the accident occurred. Police believed him because he was a congressman and had connections with a lot of powerful people.

Jason shook the thoughts of his past from his mind and grabbed Janae as she giggled and kissed him. "I love you woman," Jason said.

"I love you, too." Janae replied.

*****

"I have everything all packed up for my move. You two be sure to check on my house and make sure the maintenance people are paid regularly. If this shit doesn't work out, I'll still need to have a nice home to come back to." Taylor joked.

Trinity rubbed her belly and gave Taylor a look. "You know this is a big step. Are you really ready for this?" She asked.

"Yeah, Tay. Don't take this job just because you want to run away from Ryan. This is a life changing step, and if you're not serious, it won't work out anyway." Teagan said.

"Look, I've thought about this long and hard, and this is really what I want to do. I need to get out so that I can have my own company... continuing to work for someone else is not going to get me where I want to be. I know y'all are going to miss me; that's why you two are fussing at me. I'm going to miss y'all too." Taylor said with a grin.

"Girl, ain't nobody gon miss your irritating ass. I hope you get a life when you move to L.A." Teagan said.

"I don't know what Tea is talking about, but I'm going to miss you, lil' sis. You better make sure you fly back when I get ready to deliver your nephew." Trinity said.

Taylor nodded her head and went back to labeling her boxes with the help of her sisters. They worked for about two more hours before the sisters decided to call it a night and go home. Will came back over after they were gone to help Taylor with doing something else.

"Hey baby, how is packing going? I told you I could help you, I don't know why you had to get rid of me." Will asked.

"It went well, and we just wanted to talk. You know us. We male bash when we get together." Taylor said making Will laugh.

"Knowing y'all, yeah, you did. I can't wait to get you out to my house. I don't know why you won't just move in with me instead of renting a townhouse." Will fussed.

"I told you it's too soon for that. We'll be together all the time when I'm not working anyway, so it won't matter. You have to show me around to all of the happening places and treat me to a shopping spree on Rodeo Dr." Taylor joked.

"Absolutely baby, you got that! You can have whatever you want, too. I would just feel better knowing that every night I could go to sleep with you and every morning I could wake up to your beautiful face." Will agreed.

Taylor was joking, but she knew that Will would spoil her without hesitation. She was happy with him. It wasn't a rebound thing, but she still didn't feel for him the way she did about Ryan. That didn't mean she wasn't going to give her all in this relationship. Taylor and Will finished packing up the things she was taking with her and went to bed. Because of the fight with Lily, Todd told Taylor she didn't have to go into the office and that she could just work from home, but she needed to get some things from her office, so Taylor planned to go in to pick a few things up the next day.

Alli spotted Taylor walking into the office and damn near choked on her coffee. She turned her seat so that she could watch the action unfold. She hadn't even thought about telling Taylor that Todd had promoted Lily to a marketing executive and gave her Taylor's office, since she was busy getting herself ready for the move to L.A. as well. They had moved Taylor's things into a locker. It was Alli's last physical day in the office and she was going to have a wonderful sendoff.

Taylor tried to open the door to her office, but was stopped by the locked door. Taylor jiggled the door knob a bit and finally the door was opened. Her jaw damn near hit the floor when she saw who opened the door.

"What are you doing in my office Lily?" Taylor asked with a roll of her neck.

"Haha, you mean my office? Since you're moving on to bigger and better things, I've been promoted to a marketing exec position. I didn't graduate from college to be a secretary. I have a degree in marketing, and I plan to use it before I die. Anyway, how may I help you?" Lily asked with a snotty attitude, still sporting the black eye and bruised face Taylor had given her.

"Where are my things Lily?" Taylor asked in a condescending tone.

"Oh, they put your shit in one of the lockers in the back. Your name is on it." Lily said with a grin.

Taylor went to wrap her hand around Lily's throat but stopped herself. There was no need to put her hands on her. She had a new man and could care less about her messing around with Ryan. That shit was in the past, and Taylor had bigger and better things on her plate to deal with.

"Thanks, good luck." Taylor said before closing the door and walking towards the locker area in the back near the break room.

"Damn, I thought you were going to beat her ass like last time," Todd said. "Look, I'm sorry I moved your things without telling you. I didn't mean any disrespect by moving Lily into your office. I just hadn't thought about asking you since you were leaving in a week anyway." Todd confessed.

Taylor shook her head and grabbed her things from the locker and slammed it shut, storming out of the office towards the elevator. Alli was hot on her heels, coming to console her. She knew Taylor could put on this tough front, but deep down, she was just like any woman. Her feelings were hurt easily, and she hated to be embarrassed.

"You alright sweetie? Don't let that shit bother you. We'll be out of here in less than a week, and we won't have to deal with this messy bullshit anymore." Alli said, assuring Taylor a change was coming soon.

"Thanks Al. I'll talk to you later, and please have your shit ready when the truck comes tomorrow, unless you want to arrive before your things. Your ass will be wearing the same panties every day." Taylor joked, making Alli laugh.

Taylor continued onto the elevator and down to her car. She sat there for a while then pulled off. She decided to stop at the café to get something to eat before heading home. She grabbed a table in the back area as usual. She was eating her Cobb chicken salad when he walked in with her. He was smiling from ear to ear, looking like life was treating him well, still as fine as ever, but now, no longer hers. Ryan wrapped his arm around the woman's waist and walked her over to a table in viewing distance of where Taylor was sitting. He and the woman talked and laughed for a while before their food arrived to the table. After a while, he got up to walk towards the restroom, which was right behind the table Taylor sat at.

She tried to hide behind her menu, but that didn't work. Ryan had spotted her and stopped at her table.

"Hey beautiful! I heard that you're moving to L.A. Congrats on that. You must've really impressed Todd to get him to move you all the way over there. Usually, he's worried that his clientele would be stolen. Damn, I've missed you so much." Ryan said, sliding into the booth with Taylor.

"Hi Ryan. Yes, I'm moving, and it was Braylin's request. Otherwise, I wouldn't be going out there, but I think the change in atmosphere will be good for me. I can't wait." Taylor gushed.

"Hmph, that's good. Taylor, you know I'm really going to miss running into you, and I just wanted to tell you before you left that I really am in love with you...I love you. I only wish I was able to tell you before all of this bullshit had happened." Ryan confessed.

Taylor was shocked. Yeah, she could tell that Ryan loved her, but to hear it actually come out of his mouth meant so much more to her. She wanted to yell out that she felt the same way, but she couldn't. She didn't want to backtrack. Plus, he had a woman with him. Thinking of him with that beautiful woman got Taylor a little upset.

"Cool! Well, I don't want you leaving your date alone too long. Nice seeing you." Taylor said, throwing enough money on the table to pay for her meal and to cover the tip; she stormed out of the restaurant.

Ryan sat at the table for a moment after Taylor left, with his hands on his head. He wanted so badly to run behind her, to be able to move to L.A. with her, but he knew that he couldn't. He was going to make sure she knew that he would wait for her, no matter how long it took for her to realize that with him is where she belonged. Ryan went ahead to the restroom and came back out to the table where Alana was, sporting a fake smile.

"So, was that her?" Alana asked shocking Ryan as usual.

"Yes, that was her, but how did you know?" Ryan questioned.

"Your whole demeanor changed. You were in good spirits when you left. Now, you're back and you're looking like you lost your best friend. You know, we can cut this date short if you'd like some time to yourself." Alana said.

"Nah, time alone is definitely what I don't need. Let's enjoy the rest of our date and later we can enjoy something else." Ryan said slyly.

*****

It was the last night Taylor would be in Atlanta, and her family decided to throw her a going away party; it was packed. The party was being thrown at a big hall and was decked out. Taylor stepped out of the Bentley Coupe Will drove in an all-black fitted pencil dress with a deep cut that had gold accessories attached. Her breasts sat up, her ass poked out, and the black and gold Jimmy Choo heels made her look like a sophisticated vixen. Will walked over to her side with slim black pants and a nice black shirt with gold accents to match Taylor with black and gold Jimmy Choo sneakers. He closed the door behind her, then grabbed her hand leading her into the building.

As soon as Taylor entered the party, she was announced as the woman of the hour. They were celebrating the next big step in her life and allowing everyone to get a chance to see her before she moved to L.A. She was greeted by her mother and sisters as soon as she made it over to her VIP section. At the table next to them were Alli, Tim, a few other co-workers she was cool with, and some of their friends. Shortly after, Todd walked in with his wife and greeted everyone, giving Taylor a hug. Will pulled Taylor onto the dance floor and slow danced with her to a R. Kelly song that played, kissing her neck.

"Wow babe, you must be really special for this many people to bid you farewell. I'm just happy I'm not going to have to say goodbye to you." Will said.

Taylor rubbed the spot where her name was tatted on his chest while looking up at Will and laid her head down on it. "I'm glad about that, too. And what do you mean? I'm the shit. Everybody loves me." Taylor joked.

As the two of them continued to dance, Ryan and Alana walked in finding a seat at the table with Todd and Meghan. Alli spotted Ryan and hurriedly looked over to Taylor, who had already laid eyes on him. Ryan's eyes were trained on Taylor and caused her to look away. Her heart rate sped up, and she felt like she was going to pass out. Taylor desperately needed something to drink.

"You good baby? You're sweating. I guess I was showing out to much on this dance floor. Have a seat, and I'll get you some water." Will said with concern.

"Vodka… I need a vodka straight. Apple Cîroc please baby." Taylor said with a nervous grin.

Will walked off and Ryan walked up, as if he was waiting for him to leave. "I really need to talk to you Tay, and don't worry, I'm not trying to make a scene. I'll meet you in the room over there." Ryan told Taylor before walking off towards a back room.

Taylor knew it wasn't a good idea to be alone with Ryan or to even listen to what he had to say, but she needed this closure before she left. She needed for the both of them to be clear on where they stood. Taylor followed a few seconds behind Ryan to make sure it didn't look suspicious. She walked into room and Ryan locked the door behind her and grabbed her hand to turn her around. He looked deep into her eyes making her look away. He grabbed Taylor's chin and lifted her face towards him.

"I know why you're doing this… it's your pride, seeing me and Lily in a compromising position is forever etched into your mind. So even though you know she drugged me, and I didn't do anything with her, you can't get over it, and I get that. And I also get the fact that you have moved on, but all that doesn't stop the love I have for you. I'm a true believer in the saying, "If it's meant to be, it'll come back to you," and I believe we'll have our time again one day. So I wanted to wish you well with everything. I hope you're successful in everything you do and that you find true happiness." Ryan confessed, almost with tears in his eyes.

Taylor couldn't hold back the tears that stung her eyes. They streamed down her pretty face. "Thank you so much Ryan, for everything. I believe in that saying as well, and you're right, my pride was hurt, and the fact that she rubbed it in my face made it even worst. I've been angry, I've been fighting, and this just isn't me, so this move to L.A. just felt like the best thing for me. Leaving you… it hurts, but not because we didn't get a chance to truly see where the relationship could go, but…but because I fell in love with you in such a short period of time. I tried to fight it, and it only made the love stronger. I hope you're able to move on and that you can forget about me." Taylor said, attempting to walk away.

Ryan grabbed her hand and pulled her back into a lip-locking, tongue tangling kiss. She sucked his bottom lip as she pulled away from him, pushing him back. Taylor ran over to the mirror on the back wall of the room and dug into her purse to fix her makeup.

"No, no, no. We cannot do this Ryan, I have to go." Taylor said just above a whisper. She fixed her makeup and straightened up before leaving the room closing the door behind her.

Ryan stood there with a grin on his face. He now knew that Taylor's heart belonged to him, but she needed some time. So he was going to wait it out and use Alana to help past time until she was ready. He wiped the lipstick and makeup from his face in the mirror, straightened his collar on his shirt, then walked out of the room, walking straight back to the bathroom that was in the opposite direction of the party room, to avoid suspicion.

"Here you go, baby. Sorry it took so long, I ran into one of my old buddies over there. I didn't know Kel was your cousin." Will said, handing Taylor the Cîroc on the rocks.

Taylor hurriedly took a sip from the drink Will brought her. She couldn't believe she told Ryan the truth and that she had allowed him to kiss her. Taylor couldn't deny the attraction was still there, and even after all of the craziness, she still got butterflies when Ryan kissed her. She hated to admit that she was happy that Ryan said he would wait for her until she was ready for him. For some strange reason, she had a feeling she'd be looking for him again to sweep her off of her feet. But as the same time, Taylor felt like this shit was getting out of hand, and she couldn't wait until the next day so that she could hop on that flight to L.A. She just wanted to get the hell out of dodge before someone got hurt. Taylor gulped down the rest of the drink and looked up as Trinity and Teagan went up to get on the mic and the music was lowered.

"Today is truly bittersweet. Our best friend, our little sister is moving two thousand miles away, and we won't be able to see her as much as we'd like. But… she is moving to follow her dreams of being the best at this marketing thing and will probably make a ton of money doing it. But, Taylor deserves it. She has always been the one who would rather work on her homework or project before going outside to hang with friends, or would rather study than watch TV. Our sister loves to shop, she loves nice things, and she doesn't mind going hard to get the things she wants. She is truly a beautiful person and to know her is to love her. We're definitely going to miss you little sis. Make sure you visit as much as possible. And make sure you bring gifts when you do. To Tay Tay, we love you boo!" Trinity and Teagan said.

Thandi didn't like speaking in front of crowds when she knew she would bust out crying, so she said what she needed to in private.

"Baby, I hope you succeed at everything you set out to accomplish, and I hope that your love life makes you equally as happy. Go out there, show them what you're made of, and have fun… live your life baby!" Thandi said and hugged Taylor.

"Thank you, Mama. Having your support means so much to me. I'm so excited; I can't wait to see what's in store for me. You were right. Doing what I needed to do for me seemed to have lifted a weight from my shoulders. I'm happier, and at the same time, I feel like I'm about to go so hard in L.A. every marketing firm out there is about to have a fight on their hands." Taylor gushed.

The remainder of the party was filled with short conversations, dancing, and drinking. Alli and Tim announced that they couldn't wait to turn up in L.A. and that they weren't going to let their new boss down. Morgan showed up right before the party ended and walked over to the table where Taylor sat, clearly drunk and upset.

"You're getting a raise and a new life only because your boss and his mistress wanted you out of the picture to keep you away from Ryan and because Todd couldn't have you." Morgan said, taking everyone by surprise. "Yeah, they thought I didn't know about their lil' plan. Lily wanted Ryan and Todd wanted you. By removing you, Ryan wouldn't come around and Lily could try her luck, and with you out of the way, Ryan couldn't have you." Morgan slurred before security pulled him out of the party.

Taylor grabbed her things and walked out of the door with Will following behind her. He closed the door after she got into the car and ran around to get in. He pulled off and the tears poured from Taylor's eyes.

"I don't want to have anything to do with Atlanta; I'm never coming back. This place has brought me nothing but grief and heartache. I'm done." Taylor cried.

Will reached over and rubbed her thigh to console her before speaking, "It's okay, baby. You never have to come back here if you don't want to. Just know that I'm going to do everything in my power to make you happy and keep you that way.

The next day, Taylor, along with Alli, Will, and Tim boarded their flight to L.A. first class. She felt a like a weight had been lifted off of her shoulder and if starting her own firm was only an idea she had pushed to the back of her mind, it was definitely something that was going to happen as soon as possible now, after hearing what Morgan said last night. They say a drunk mind speaks sober thoughts, so she had no reason not to believe what Morgan was saying, and in a way, it all seemed to make sense. Todd had been too nice, and Lily was too damn comfortable. Hell, they had messed around before so it was no reason why they weren't conspiring to hurt us both.

"This is it baby, the start of our new beginning. I love you." Will said.

Taylor's eyes bucked out of her head, she smiled and said, "I love you, too, baby." She did have love for Will, but she wasn't in love with him. She was just going to play everything by ear. Life would be different in L.A. She wasn't going to overthink everything, torturing herself with things that were out of her control, she was going to live life like she lived twice. She wasn't going to second-guess herself anymore.

Chapter Ten

They landed at 12 in the afternoon and were met at the airport in L.A. by Braylin's team, who helped to secure each of them a townhome in a nice area, in Hollywood. With Kragin & Smith covering room and board for the three months they'd be there, they were able to live well, even though Taylor would be good either way. Taylor parted ways with Tim and Alli before they left the airport. Taylor would go with Will to his place to pick up a car for her to use while she was there and to allow him to handle a few things. The others were being taken to their new homes and to get rentals.

They pulled up to Will's house and Taylor's jaw dropped. Will's house was like a glass house on a private hill. He had an infinity pool, a huge house and acres of private land. Taylor knew Will was successful, but she didn't know he was balling like this. His house and property looked like something off of the show "Cribs." Taylor followed Will through the house in amazement, when his phone rung and he said he had to take the call.

"It's Sko, wassup? Absolutely! This is Sko you're talking to. We don't do $1 million deals. Tell them they have to come better than that. That's right, have them call me when they get their heads screwed on straight. Thanks." Will said before hanging up the phone. "You good, baby? You ready to see your new car?" Will asked.

Taylor's eyes lit up before she spoke, then her face turned serious. "Baby, what is it that you do again? You're not a drug dealer are you?" She asked, making Will laugh.

"Hell no! Haha, I can't believe you asked me that. You really don't know?" Will asked.

"I was only told you were a business owner, that's it. I never thought to ask you when you were spending all of that money on me and bouncing me on your dick, soo now I wanna know." Taylor said with a grin.

"I'm a real estate broker. I buy and flip homes in areas like this, so I do have a construction/interior decorating company, and I own one of the hottest restaurants on Rodeo Dr. That's it! Everything I have, I've earned it legally and every deal I do is legal. Don't worry, I don't want to go to jail, and I don't want you to either." Will said reassuring Taylor.

"Okay, now back to this car." Taylor said in a matter of fact tone.

Will laughed and led Taylor to the back of the house where there was a long garage that housed about six cars. He pressed a button on a remote, lifting the door that protected the 2016 Bentley Continental GT V8 S convertible in candy apple red, one of Taylor's favorite colors. He handed her the key fob and watched her run and hop in the car, then get back out when she realized he had gotten the car for her. Will had her initials embroidered into the headrest of the seats instead of the Bentley signature.

"Oh my god, Sko! You should not have done that. What if we don't work out?" Taylor spat, wishing she had never said that. But it was too late, she couldn't take it back.

"There's one thing that you should know after knowing me for so many years. I'm not a petty nigga. I don't care about that. If we work, then I'm beyond happy. If we don't, then I'll learn from this experience, and it would definitely be a love lost, but for now, let's just live for the moment." Will said making Taylor smile.

She hugged him then jumped in her new car. Will followed her in a Bugatti to the subdivision where the townhome was. She pulled up and pressed the button on the remote to the garage Elle, Braylin's assistant, had given her. It was a two-car garage, so they were both able to store the cars there and walk into the house from the garage, which led them into the mudroom/laundry room. Taylor and Will toured the huge three bedroom/three bathroom townhome that was furnished with new furniture that matched Taylor's taste to a T.

"Damn, they told us the places would be unfurnished. I must've gotten lucky." Taylor exclaimed.

"Word?" Will said.

"Hold on, you did this?" Taylor asked, then pushed Will onto the couch and started kissing him.

She got up and undressed herself before walking to the master bedroom. Taylor slid the door to the shower open and turned on the water. Will followed her in, lifting her onto the wall and sliding into her slowly. He covered her mouth with his and stroked her deeply.

"God Sko! Ooh baby, you're so deep!" Taylor cried out.

"Mm-hmm, take this dick. You love daddy dick, don't you?" Will grunted.

"Ooh yes, Daddy, I love it! Damn!" Taylor moaned.

"You love daddy, don't you?" Will asked, sucking on Taylor's bottom lip.

"I LOVE DADDY SO MUCH!" Taylor screamed out.

Taylor's eyes rolled into the back of her head and her head leaned back onto the wall as Will served her up a pleasurable dish of punishment. He let her down onto her feet upon her command, and Taylor pushed him back onto the wall, falling to her knees to admire the long, thick piece of chocolate she had before her. Her mouth began to water as the shower rained down on them. Taylor sucked Will's dick into her mouth like a vacuum taking him deep down her throat without gagging. She massaged his balls while sucking him and making her throat vibrate on his dick.

"Tay goddamit, baby!" Will panted, barely able to speak. Taylor bobbed on his dick like her life depended on it, forcing Will to cry out. "Ooh baby, I'm cumming!" Will belted.

Taylor swallowed every drop he served her and got up wiping her mouth and licking her lips, with a grin. Taylor knew just how to make Will feel good, and she loved knowing how to satisfy him. She smiled at Will once he was able to compose himself and look back at her with a smile.

"You good baby? You need a minute?" Taylor asked cockily.

"Ooh, you're going to pay for that." Will promised.

He got down on his knees and wrapped Taylor's legs around his head and started to kiss on her bald, pretty pussy. His tongue parted her lips and found her swollen clit throbbing with anticipation. He gently pulled it into his mouth and used his fingers to maximize the pleasure she felt. Will's tongue moved like a tornado, forcing her to take the tongue lashing he was putting on her. She was scratching his scalp and shaking like she was twerking on Will's face. Taylor's head laid up against the wall, and when she couldn't take anymore, she shook her head like she was in the exorcist.

"OH MY GOD, SKO, PLEASE BABY, OOOOH!" Taylor screamed.

Taylor was squirting like she was in one of those videos on the porn sites and Will was drinking down her essence just as quickly as it ran down his chin. He finally let her down from her punishment, helping her to stand up; her legs were wobbly and weak. They washed their bodies, then went to bed for a few hours. They woke up to Tim and Alli ringing the doorbell like they were crazy. Taylor stumbled out of the bed and snatched the door open.

"Girl, what the hell you want?" Taylor shouted. "Come in, damn!" She fussed.

"We haven't eaten anything. We were busy unpacking. We wanted to know if y'all wanted to go out to eat with us." Tim replied with a chuckle.

Tim and Alli laughed at Taylor being snappy with them. They could tell she had been fucking. Her hair was all over her head from getting wet in the shower. They followed her into the living room where she told them to wait on her until she got Will up so that he could go with them to get something to eat.

"Um…how the hell did you get a furnished place? That muthafuckin' Todd didn't furnish ours." Alli fussed.

"Well, my man had this done for me. And I have to show you my car he got me. My man is the shit!" Taylor bragged walking down the stairs, pulling on a sweater with Will trailing behind her.

"Hey Sko! I see you put my friend to bed early huh?" Alli said with a sinister grin.

Will laughed and followed them out the door; he and Taylor got into his Bugatti and led them to his restaurant on Rodeo Dr. The scene was lit and there were plenty of celebrities swarming the area when they arrived at Kaleb's. The wait was long for others, but they were walked right into the restaurant.

"Baby, this is really nice. It's huge and you still have a long wait? The food has to be excellent for people to be waiting all the way out of the door for this place." Taylor said, looking around the restaurant.

"Damn, there's Braylin." Alli said, getting up with Tim and Taylor in tow.

"Hey, how are you?" Alli asked.

"Oh my goodness, you all finally arrived. We were going to invite you out, but Elle said you three may be tired after that long flight and unpacking. This is my favorite restaurant,. You'll love the food here." Braylin said.

"That's great! This is my boyfriend's restaurant," Taylor said, pointing over to Will. He lifted his glass and nodded his head to acknowledge Braylin.

"Oh my goodness, that's great! So, will you all be ready to work tomorrow?" Braylin asked.

"Of course, we're not slackers, that's why we're here. My team and I are looking into starting our own firm and to do that, we need to make sure we bust our asses putting you out there." Taylor confessed.

Braylin gave a grin, satisfied that Taylor at least thought about going after what was important to her and putting her happiness first. The interest that Braylin showed in Taylor was genuine; she saw something in her the first time they met, and she was going to continue to keep her motivated until she reached her full potential and was successful in doing so.

The group enjoyed dinner then parted ways to head home and prepare for work the next day. After getting things set up for Braylin, the first thing Taylor was doing was using her connections to meet with different brands to gain their trust and business. She didn't want to waste a lot of time waiting to do what she knew she was set to do anyway and that was branch away from the company that used her for their own personal gain.

The next day was set up with meetings with new stores and private websites to market Braylin's videos and books. Taylor also had to set up a promotional tour throughout California to get the west coast familiar with the program Braylin was going to have on TV soon. They had already completed the east coast, southern and Midwestern areas. Taylor got home after a hard day of working, relaxed on the couch, and watched some TV. Will came over shortly after to bring Taylor some dinner and gave her a full body massage.

"Ooh baby, that feels so good. Thank you so much for taking care of me. I worked myself like a damn slave today. If Braylin doesn't succeed, then it just wasn't meant to be, because I've been going in for her. Her contract with Kragin & Smith ends in one week, and I'm purposely trying to drag my feet with my new outlets for her. She's going to be using Powers & Associates in another week, and I want to make sure these new huge deals bring in enough revenue for us to secure an actual location for us to open our office. We have to get a nice spot over in Hollywood, which would be the perfect spot for us." Taylor boasted.

"Damn babe, so you just stole their client?" Will asked with a chuckle.

"Hell yeah; it's a dog eat dog world. When you fuck over Taylor Powers, you fuck over yourself." Taylor said playfully.

Will laughed and shook his head at Taylor as he continued to rub his hands over her body and plant kisses in between rubs.

"You know you don't have to worry about finding a spot for you to open your firm. Your man got you babe. I'm going to look into finding you a location tomorrow… big enough for about ten people. You should really think about setting up interviews to hire the best people for your business. By the way, baby, I'm going to be really busy in the next couple of weeks. We just purchased three houses, and we're remodeling, and it's going to take up all of my time. I hate to leave you hanging like this, but I promise, as soon as we get some free time, we're going to leave the country and go on a trip. Is that cool?" Will asked trying to suck up.

"Yeah, that's cool baby. Paris is beautiful around this time of year," Taylor grinned, then looked back at him.

"If Paris is what you want, then Paris is what you'll get. Just give me a little time to get my work done." Will said planting a kiss on her lips.

*****

Will had been right, he and Taylor had barely seen each other in the past week, and she was starting to feel lonely. He had done such a good job of keeping her in good spirits and keeping her motivated to bust her ass with her new endeavors. Taylor was bored, she sat on the couch flicking through channels, unable to find anything worth watching on TV, which was why she invited Alli over to help past time.

She came over bearing gifts, too; she had a bottle of Cîroc and a few blunts of Kush.

"Damn girl, what you trying to do, have a party or something? I guess I'll have a little bit, just to help you get rid of it," Taylor replied, making Alli laugh.

"So how are you liking L.A. so far?" Alli asked, sparking the blunt and taking a few pulls.

"It's been good so far. I haven't thought about the shit that happened in ATL, and I've been having so much fun. I just feel so free out here... like I can do anything I set my mind to. I'm so glad you guys decided to come with me, and I promise I'm going to go as hard as I can to make sure we're good once we split from KRAGIN & SMITH." Taylor said, grabbing the blunt from Alli.

"I have no doubt that we're going to win. I've already secured some new business for us. Since you know I'm a makeup fanatic, MAC is willing to sit down with us and go over some plans for its new line that will feature one of those popular actresses. The meeting is in a week, but you know I have already started on it, and I'll need you and Tim to help out." Alli said.

"Oh my god, Al, that's great! That's what I'm talking about. We're out here making shit happen already. You know when they said you were out sucking dick to make it, I didn't believe them. No seriously, how the hell did you land that meeting?" Taylor questioned.

"Well, let's just say this mouth does a little more than just talking." Alli said playfully.

"Eww bitch, and you got me smoking with you? Hand me that liquor so I can wash this sin from my lips." Taylor said with an ugly face, causing Alli to bust out in laughter.

"Damn, I was just kidding! We don't do that at Powers &Associates. We're all about showing and proving. Our work will speak volumes and draw in those sugar daddies I'll need to buy me a new house and car." Alli said, clearly high as a kite and Taylor who was giggling like a giddy school girl.

"I did meet this basketball player from Golden State or the Lakers, one of those damn teams. Let's just say he signed more than my poster. That big mufucka had my legs posted up like I was flexible or some shit. Girl, he was treating my ass like a human pretzel. I was so sore when I left that hotel room, I couldn't even steal the shampoo and lotion. I did snap a few pictures of him sleep and us in bed together, just in case his ass is married. He's fine, though. We're going out again tomorrow. I told his ass I hope he pays like he weighs." Alli said making Taylor laugh.

Taylor was crying laughing, "Ooh, you're so damn stupid. I can't with you Al. You gon blackmail the man?" She said.

"Hell yeah, if he ever try to fuck over me! I'm gon have his ass on Facebook, the Gram, everywhere, throw it back and have his ass on Myspace. I ain't mufuckin playing." Alli said seriously.

The doorbell rang scaring the hell out of both Taylor and Alli. They had just sparked their second blunt and were nervous as hell. Taylor was using her hands to fan the smoke as she walked to be door and Alli was still sitting on the couch smoking, while trying to fan the smoke.

"Girl that might be him coming to get my ass for taking those pictures." Alli said nervously, making Taylor stumble to the door in laughter.

Taylor looked through the peephole, then opened the door to let Janae in; she walked in and shook her head at Taylor and Alli, laughing at their silliness. Janae walked in with her small belly showing through her shirt, wearing her hair in a ponytail that was pulled back.

"Tay, you know while you're trying to fan the smoke your friend is still back there smoking, right?" Janae said pointing at Alli, Taylor turned around and started laughing.

"Ah damn. Anyway, hey boo. I wasn't expecting you, what are you doing here?" Taylor asked, giving Janae a hug.

"Oh, Jason had some last minute business out here. He wasn't going to bring me, but I begged and did a few other things, and he decided to bring me along. Plus, I wanted to surprise you, but I've missed my bestie!" Janae exclaimed.

"I've missed you, too. We were just relaxing after working so hard this week. How have things been with the baby and Jason?" Taylor asked, leading Janae back to the living room.

"We're doing great, show me around." Janae asked.

"Don't mind me, I'll be over here smoking. You two go ahead." Alli said with sarcasm.

"Good, you just relax boo." Janae said with a roll of her eyes.

Taylor led Janae upstairs to see all of the rooms and the rest of the house.

"Look, Ryan is here with us as well and he wants us to check on you. He said he won't bother you, but he had to know how things were turning out for you. They're in some kind of business meeting, so I took a cab over. Tay, I think you should give Ryan another chance." Janae confessed.

Taylor rolled her eyes before speaking, "I'm with Will, we're happy, and I'm not giving him another chance. If that's why you really came here, you can leave." Taylor spat.

She walked back downstairs, gave Alli a look and picked up her phone to make a call. "Tim, I need you to do me a favor please. Can you take Janae back to her hotel room? Thanks, I owe you big time." Taylor said before hanging up.

"You can wait out on the porch, Tim only lives next door. It was good seeing you Janae, I'll talk to you later." Taylor said opening the door and waving at Tim who was sitting in the driveway waiting on Janae.

Taylor watched as Janae waddled over to the car, then slammed the door behind her. The nerve of her friend to come all the way across the country to tell her that dumb shit; Janae had pissed her off. And to think she had been doing so good before Janae came. She hadn't thought once about Ryan or anything that had happened that night before she left. Taylor grabbed her glass of Cîroc and chugged it down.

"Damn, girl, you good? What was that about? I knew the moment her negative ass walked in it was going to be an issue. She's messy as hell and has the nerve to call me ghetto," A concerned Alli said, shaking her head.

"It was nothing worth repeating. I actually thought she was coming here as my best friend to check up on me and to make sure I was settling well. It seems like her little visit had an ulterior motive. Now, hand me that blunt." Taylor said, taking a long pull and leaning back on the couch before she exhaled.

This was exactly why Taylor wanted to leave her home; she was tired of everyone trying to push her into doing things they wanted her to do. She wanted to just live her life and decide her next move for herself. No matter what the outcome may have been. Taylor shook her head. took a few more long pulls, and laid her head back, blowing the smoke out into the air.

*****

"If you're wanting to purchase this property, we can definitely draw up some plans for the house and show you a virtual design of what it will look like after the renovations. For this house, the asking price is $1.5 million, before renovations. Depending on what you want this place to look like, that price can go up significantly." Will said.

He was having a late meeting with a potential buyer. Emily was new to L.A.; she had just graduated from college and was looking to purchase a house in the hills. Will wasn't going to go to the meeting since he was finally done handling his other business and couldn't wait to get to Taylor; he missed her. However, this client was talking about purchasing in cash and was looking to lock in on this location and start the renovations as soon as next week, so Will couldn't pass up on the offer. Plus, they were going to pay for the house and cover half the cost of the renovations up front.

"My client would like to sign the contract today. Here are the floor plans she had for this house. Since the floor plans were available on your website, she was able to go in and design the house herself. She just needs your company to sell her the house and make the changes. Do we have a deal?" Her attorney said.

"Absolutely! We have a deal and we'll get started as soon as possible. Thanks again for your business, and we'll be in touch." Will said with a smile.

He couldn't wait to get home to celebrate with Taylor. She was going to be his wife soon enough and this was exactly the type of good news they needed to add to everything positive they were trying to build. Taylor had finally started to unwind and enjoy being in L.A. with him, they were enjoying each other, and he felt like she was starting to feel for him the way he felt for her. He was planning to go out the next day to look for a ring for Taylor. She was exactly what he wanted in a wife; she had values, she worked hard, she was beautiful, smart, and she made him happy without needing to sleep with him. When Taylor chose him over Ryan, he was elated. He knew that he had to do everything in his power to show her why she had made the right choice. Once he was done printing up the contracts, they were signed and he was out the door and on his way to Taylor with a smile no one could wipe away.

*****

"Braylin, I'll need you to sign this contract for this Macy's. You'll do exclusive releases for your swimwear line with them, and they're going to market your products like crazy. They want to set up a commercial shoot for next week, and we'll need you to make sure you have several pieces prepared for that commercial. Also, Amazon is allowing you to do a contest for the release of your next book. We're wanting to give away a full month nutrition plan, along with a signed copy of the book they purchase. How does that sound?" Taylor asked not looking up from her work.

"That sounds great! Anything else boss lady?" Braylin asked with a grin.

Taylor had finally looked up and laughed at Braylin. The past week had been nothing but work for her, and because Will had also been busy with work, she was in desperate need of some TLC. Taylor wrapped up her day with Braylin and her team then headed home. This week had proven to her that she had made the right decision. She had met so many new people through Will and Tim, and had secured so many new clients, that she didn't have to worry about splitting from KRAGIN & SMITH; she was going to knock them out of the ballpark.

Once Braylin's contract was over with KRAGIN & SMITH, Todd had been calling Taylor trying to get her to convince Braylin to sign on with them for a year. See, the initial contract she had signed was only for three months, and since she had been burned in the past by other companies, her team had come up with an idea to deal with new companies under a 3-month preliminary contract. If things went well, they'd resign with a longer contract. Although Kragin & Smith had done more than any other company had, it was the work of Taylor alone that had gotten everything done. Without her, she knew they wouldn't have a chance in the world of keeping her happy, so Braylin decided to follow her dream child. She signed a one-year contract with Power & Associates; the same day, her contract with KRAGIN & SMITH ended.

To say that Todd was unhappy about Taylor, Alli, and Tim quitting the firm was an understatement. Todd had called them everything but the child of God in text messages and emails. It was Todd's own underhanded tricks had come back to bite him in the ass. He didn't realize that his contract with Braylin would be up in a month when he made the deal and signed contracts to send Taylor and her team away with her for three months. Nowhere in his contract did he force Taylor to remain an employee to ensure Braylin would continue to do business with him. And once Teagan read over the contract for Taylor, she let her know that she was okay to start her own company and to take Braylin with her. The contract only stated that for the remainder of Braylin's contract, Taylor and her team would remain her sole marketing team and Todd had agreed to that and to pay for everything for three months. When Taylor found this out, she knew that Morgan had been telling the truth all along; it was clearly a rushed contract and they lost in the end.

Taylor pulled up and decided to leave her car in the driveway, since she had planned on going back out to get something to eat. She unlocked the door and dropped her purse on the floor; the entire living room was filled with roses. Pink, white, and red roses adorned the room, and there was a card attached to one of the bouquets. Taylor opened the card and read it aloud.

I know you've been working hard, so here's something special for a special lady...follow the trail to your treat.

Taylor automatically assumed it was Will doing something special for her since he knew how tired she was from the talk they'd had earlier. She hadn't really spent time with him this week, so this was just what she was needing to unwind for the weekend. There were rose petals along with candles that led her to a tub filled with a hot bubble bath. There was a bottle of Ace and two filled champagne flutes sitting on the side of the tub. The water had to have been ran within a few minutes' time, because it was still hot when Taylor stuck her hand into the tub. The TV in the master bedroom played Pandora's Love songs station. R. Kelly's Sextime.

Taylor smiled and picked up one of the flutes and drank down a glass of the Ace, then refilled her glass, before deciding to undress and slide into the tub underneath the bubbles in the hot water. She took a sip from the flute and laid back closing her eyes. This was exactly what she needed. This was the reason why she was starting to feel like she was falling for Will. He had been everything to her that she thought she had found with Ryan and slowly but surely, he had started to win over her heart. Taylor couldn't stop the grin that formed on her face as she thought about Will's hands touching her and his mouth tasting her. She was startled when she caught Ryan massaging her hand and rubbing her arm. Taylor thought she was dreaming when she stood up in the tub. She blinked a few times, still seeing Ryan in front of her.

"Ryan, what are you doing here?" Taylor exclaimed.

"I tried to wait for you to come back to me, but it's taking too long. I've missed you Tay, and I want you back. And I'm not leaving until you come home with me." Ryan confessed.

"Baby, what's going on? The door was unlocked and I…" Will said before stopping and seeing a naked Taylor standing in front of Ryan.

"Baby, it's not what you think…" Taylor said, trying to make sense of what was happening.

How the fuck am I going to get out of this?

To be continued…

Text Shan to 22828 to stay up to date with new releases, sneak peeks, contest, and more…
Check your spam if you don't receive an email thanking you for signing up.

Text SPROMANCE to 22828 to stay up to date on new releases, plus get information on contest, sneak peeks, and more!